D1706671

W. G. Scott

BILLY WEIRD

For Michelle

Billy Weird

© 2023 by W.G.Scott

All rights reserved.

First Edition

ISBN: 9798856411125

Illustrations by Mallory Terrell

Layout by Prest Design

At the urging of others, I have decided to write this book. I always assumed that I had lived a fairly normal life until I began telling stories from my childhood and beyond to others. My listeners were always amazed at the strange goings on in my neck of the woods and could not believe the outlandishly hilarious stories from my past. I, more than anyone else, can hardly believe that I survived all of the antics and down right stupid circumstances that I often placed myself in during my childhood and teen years.Please read with an open mind, understanding that things were far different in the 1960s and 70s than they are now.

Contents

1

Heartache and Birth

I was born ten days after my uncle's suicide. My dad's younger brother, Uncle Bill—whom I was named after—was experiencing a challenging time in his life. He was thirty-four years old, single, and a military veteran of WWII. Not long after leaving the military, Uncle Bill was involved in a barroom fight that left him with several health issues, the least of which was epileptic seizures. Some of my family members told me that Uncle Bill might have been making sexual advances toward another man in the bar that night and that the other man went crazy on him and broke a beer bottle on his head. The resulting brain injury was what caused the epilepsy.

Uncle Bill's health issues prevented him from working and supporting himself, so he was living with his mother. He had far too much time on his hands to dwell on how hopeless his life seemed to be. On a cold, snowy day in December 1958, he took his handgun, pointed it at the center of his chest, and pulled the trigger. Over the next several minutes as his life ebbed away, legend has it, he had second thoughts about what he'd just done. But the bullet had severed his aorta; he bled out and lost consciousness.

It's been said, "*Suicide is a permanent solution to a temporary problem.*" There is always hope. How disheartening and troubling that no one was there to show him, even in the bleakest of circumstances. What a gut-wrenching experience it must have been for my dad and mom. Prior to his death, Uncle Bill told Mom that if she had a baby boy, she just had to name him Bill. She was true to her word and named me William but always called me Billy!

I was the sixth of eight children made up of four boys and four girls. Because I was the youngest boy, my dad often referred to me as his baby boy. Eighteen years from my birth, I would go through a transformation that would change me forever. The uncanny life that awaited me would be anything but normal by most people's standards. Looking back and reflecting on all the wild and idiotic episodes of my life, I am thoroughly amazed that I am still alive and kicking. No one can see the future, so seemingly without a care, my parents welcomed me into this world even though their hearts had been broken.

When Mom brought me home from the hospital, she found a 1958 Mercury Head dime lodged in my belly button. She saved the dime, and I am still in possession of it. The nurses placed it there so that my belly button would be an innie instead of an outie.

The birth order of us eight is as follows: Ruby, Leroy, Archie, Vernie, Cameron, two years later, me, then two more sisters, Helga and Monica. With so many children in his wake, my father was often asked if we were Roman Catholics, and he always replied, "No, just passionate Baptists."

My poor mother was pregnant for almost a solid twenty years. Within that twenty-year span, she experienced one miscarriage and gave birth to a full-term, stillborn baby. My oldest sister is now eighty and my youngest sister is sixty. At the time of this writing,

2022, we are all still alive. Several of my siblings were born barely a year apart. My dad had a real thing for my mom (he called her Maddie). Birth control options were minimal back in the 1950s and 60s. Mom gave birth to my youngest sister in 1961 when she was forty years old. While still in the hospital after delivery, she told my newly married, oldest sister, Ruby, "This baby should have been yours!" One year later to the day, Ruby gave birth to her first little one. Several people in my family have the same birthday. With so many aunts, uncles, and cousins this was bound to happen.

When Ruby got married and moved out of the house, that left seven kids and two parents in a single-story, 900-square-foot house with one actual bedroom and a very small bathroom. It was the beginning of the freewheeling 1960s which ushered in the chaos that reigned in our tiny cottage.

2

Sounds From the Attic

Living in a 900-square-foot house with nine people sounds awful but this was our life. And for me as a kid, it was normal. Our sleeping arrangements consisted of two sets of bunkbeds situated in what was more a large closet than a bedroom. There was barely enough space for the bunkbeds on each side of the small room with about a two-foot walkway between them. That took care of sleeping arrangements for four of us. While I took a bottom bunk, Cameron was in the bunkbed above me. Many nights a loud *thud* woke me, and then the crying would start. Cameron, while sound asleep, had rolled out of the top bunk and smacked the hard carpet-less floor once again. How she managed this on so many occasions without a single broken bone was a wonder. Parallel, about two feet away was the other set of bunkbeds on which Archie slept in the top bunk and Vernie was in the bottom bunk. Sometimes we removed the bedding from all the bunkbeds—even though it made Mom angry—and placed it on the top bunks. Then most of us would hide on the top bunks and wait for Monica, who was about two years old at the time, to walk into the room. We called for Monica to come find us. When she stepped into our tiny bedroom, we would holler "Pygmy!" and throw all the bedding on top of her. She loved it! We lovingly referred to her as a pygmy because she was so little and cute and would squeal with delight as the blankets, pillows, and sheets rained down on her.

The only actual bedroom in our home was where my mom and dad and two younger sisters slept. My parents were in a full-sized bed and Monica slumbered in a baby bed while Helga snoozed on a folding cot. On stormy nights, my parents would end up with two or three frightened children huddled in bed with them. Dad often complained about a certain child who would snuggle up next to him on those stormy nights and wet the bed. He was never pleased with that and often reminded that child about it. We won't mention any names to protect the innocent.

My oldest brother, Leroy slept in the living room on a sleeper sofa, and we all envied him for that. He had an entire room to himself. He was a senior in high school when I was a first grader, and I always looked up to him. He was the tallest of my brothers.

My most terrifying memory of living in that tiny house was the scratching and clawing sounds coming from the attic after dusk. Each evening after sunset, my father bellowed, "You kids go to sleep!" We eventually quieted down and then the scratching noise in the attic would start up. I vividly recall lying awake on most nights in a state of absolute terror over what was living and scurrying across our attic. I was about four years old when my older brothers told me that the noise coming from the attic was *rats*! Not just ordinary rats but the kind of rats that sneak out of the attic at night to feed. They convinced me that if they could not find food, they would chew my face off while I slept! I spent countless sleepless nights listening to the rats clambering through the attic while I hid under my blankets. I figured if I stayed awake, they wouldn't eat my face off. When I did sleep, I had nightmares about rats clawing and biting me while my heart pounded in my chest. I woke up in a panic, drenched in sweat.

Leroy, seventeen at the time, had a plan on how to rid our home of those monstrous creatures. The rats would venture out of the attic and enter our tiny furnace room at night, so we always kept that door closed. Leroy designed a rattrap that would catch several rats at the same time. His blueprint involved a large cardboard box with tall sides open at the top, dry dog food for bait, a three-foot-long 2x4 for an entry ramp and a thirty-six-inch Louisville Slugger wooden baseball bat. Leroy put a small amount of dog food in the bottom of the cardboard box and leaned the 2x4 against the outside of the box so that the rats could crawl up the ramp and jump into the box to eat the dry dog food. The sides of the box were so tall that the rats couldn't jump high enough to get back out. Leroy would set up his trap before bed, and we would inspect it early the next morning for vermin.

I concealed my four-year-old self behind my big brother for safety as he quietly opened the furnace door. The moment the door was opened, and light entered the dark furnace room, the rats would feverishly claw at the sides of the cardboard box trying to escape. Chills ran up and down my young spine while I had a death grip on my oldest brother's pant leg. There were always three of us that checked the rattrap: Leroy, me, and his thirty-six-inch Louisville Slugger. He used the big end of that baseball bat and thumped every rat found in the box on the head killing each one. I peered over the top of the box to view the massacre. It was frightening to the max for a four-year-old! There was scratching and clawing and blood, then silence. It was the end of another successful hunt. Those sights and sounds of my childhood still haunt me in my dreams. Rats reproduce at an alarming rate, and there was never a shortage of them in our home.

3

Bucket of Worms

Growing up in the hills and wooded countryside with so many siblings was an experience in and of itself. Most days we ran wild through the woods surrounding our home, and more often than not, we were barefoot. Our biggest concern with running barefoot was trying to avoid cuts and bruises on our feet. The bottoms of my feet were so toughened up that I could easily run shoeless on the gravel road with little to no pain. That ability always impressed my father who informed me that he couldn't *walk* barefoot let alone *run* barefoot on that rough gravel. It did help that I was small and weighed so little. We never considered the possibility of parasites invading our bodies, some of which enter through your feet. Who knew?

Archie found out the hard way what a parasite invasion was all about. He had woken up one Friday morning and was getting ready for school when he noticed something strange in his underwear. There appeared to be a small worm wiggling in his undies—which was not a body part. He asked Mom what it was, and she flew into a full-on panic. She assumed that Archie had either hookworms or pinworms. You could become affected with hookworms from walking barefoot in soil contaminated with the larvae. Pinworms, on the other hand, lay eggs around the anus at night. Others can contract them by coming into contact with the eggs left on clothing, bedding and other materials. Whichever worm it was didn't matter; they were both nasty. Archie was eleven years old at the time and thought that he was about to give up the ghost. Mom assured him that he would be just fine and that she could rid his body of those invaders on Saturday. This took place in 1964 and the cure seemed like one of those home remedies that would be better left to a real doctor. Living in the country, away from civilization, made us very independent, and we took care of most everything ourselves. There was no YouTube to ask how to get rid of worms, but somehow Mom knew a way.

In our small home, we had one minuscule bathroom. There was a toilet, sink and a tiny metal three-foot-by-three-foot shower in one corner. Yes, one bathroom for nine people! Many times, I showered with two older brothers and stood in the corner of the shower with my hands over my face, waiting for them to wash and get out. I envied kids that had no siblings, and I've since learned the irony that the only child envies someone like me for having so many brothers and sisters. Archie was not looking forward to his procedure and had no clue what was about to occur. He had real angst worrying about what would happen to him on Saturday. Dr. Mom assured him that she would take good care of him. Better him than me!

On the day of Archie's procedure, there were plenty of spectators. Vernie, Cameron, Helga, and I were all interested in Archie's fate. Monica was too young to understand and not interested in the least. Back in that day and time we received only three channels on our television, which were 4, 5, and 9. This real-life episode was going to be far better than any television show. The festivities were to take place in our tiny bathroom, and Mom continued to tell us to get out and stay out, but we kept sneaking back to peek. Mom placed a five-gallon metal bucket in the tiny shower and informed Archie that he would be using that bucket instead of the toilet. At this point in the proceedings, he was still clueless. He was purposely kept in the dark about his impending procedure so that he wouldn't flee into the woods and hide. Dr. Mom's other medical equipment consisted of a rubber hot water bottle, a three-foot-long hose that was attached to the hot water bottle, and a nozzle that fit on the opposite end of the hose. Archie was especially skeptical of that nozzle. The liquid that Mom put into that hot water bottle was some powerful stuff. She had Archie take off all his clothes and stand in front of the bucket in the small shower. He was instructed to bend over and hold on to the sides of the bucket. Dr. Mom then oiled up the nozzle and inserted it into my poor brother's keister. This assault on his personal space irritated him, and he was very vocal about it. She told him to hold still while she filled his bowels with what he must have thought was rocket fuel. The pressure was building as his rear end received the liquid propellant and Mom told him he had to hold it until a minute was up. His cries for help resonated from that empty bucket but fell on deaf ears. She told him that when the minute was up, she would remove the nozzle, and he could use the bucket. That was the longest sixty seconds of his young life. Mom continued to holler, "You kids get out of here!", but we were not missing this for all the tea in China. As Mom spun Archie around—to direct his rear end over the bucket—and removed that nozzle, the blastoff started. Boy did he let loose with some serious pressure. It sounded like a firehose shooting into the bottom of that metal bucket. The look on Archie's face said all that needed to be said. I thought at one point he was going to take off and crash into the ceiling. He rode that bucket for quite some time, holding both sides with a death grip. When it was over, someone had to inspect the contents. *Ick, ick, ick!* This was like witnessing a car crash you shouldn't look at, but just had too anyway. Along with the liquid and everything else in the bucket, there were tiny white worms twitching all over the place. *EEEWWW!* No one can say my life has been boring. I was only five years old and had already seen things most people would never see, and I took it all in stride. That was not commonplace in the average American household. Even to this day, it takes a whole lot to gross me out because I have seen way too much. Archie was always the skinniest of all us kids growing up, and I remember thinking he might just need another procedure.

4

Dog Food

Along with a passion for fishing, my dad took great pleasure in quail hunting. We raised quail in a small pen, and he used the quail to train bird dogs. As each of us boys grew old enough, it was our inherited job to feed and water Dad's bird dogs. At around twelve years of age, the task was passed to the next son in line. When Archie inherited this task, I was around five years old and gullible. I loved to accompany my older brother to the dog pen. Originally a chicken house with a tin roof, it worked great for dogs, and was about fifty yards from the house. It was a short walk, but just far enough that unsupervised adolescents could get into trouble.

Sunny summer days in the middle of America were like any other with us bored preteens looking for something to occupy our time. This was way before home computers and video games, and my dad was daily yelling, "You kids get outside!" Outside was the place to be in the summertime. I foolishly looked up to my older brothers and paid the price many times for that homage.

In a separate instance, I watched as Archie climbed upon the roof of our house carrying an umbrella. I asked him what he was doing, and he said he was going to fly like Mary Poppins. It all sounded reasonable to me as I stood there on the ground, waiting for him to make the leap off the roof. He opened the umbrella and yelled, "Geronimo!" When he leapt from the roof while holding the umbrella above his head, he dropped straight down about eight or nine feet, colliding with the ground. The umbrella turned inside out on the way down, and he did a real number on his ankles when he smacked the ground with a thud and loud groan. He walked kind of funny for about a week because both of his ankles were swollen. You'd have thought that I would have learned not to follow in his footsteps after the Mary Poppins incident, but I didn't.

One memorable day, I followed Archie out to the dog pen. We carried two fifteen-ounce cans of Vets dog food to feed our two bird dogs. My brothers had a system for opening those cans, and it was handed down from one brother to another. The trick was to open both ends of the can with a can opener and push the canned horse meat out into the dog bowl. If you just opened one end of the can, the suction wouldn't allow the horse meat to plop out into the bowl. The bonus was with both ends gone from the empty cans, we could stomp the cans flat and use them for frisbees. Those flat square pieces of metal flying through the air were dangerous, and we weren't very smart for throwing those at one another.

The day's dog feeding ritual took an unusual turn when Archie opened one end of a can. Before he opened the other end, he stuck his fingers in the can and started eating the horse meat—at least he had me convinced that he was eating it and that it tasted delicious. He exclaimed, "No wonder these dogs go crazy for this food; it tastes really good." One would consider that even a five-year-old would be intelligent enough not to fall for that. I just wasn't that astute, and Archie convinced me to stick my fingers into the can and try some for myself. It had to be luscious because those dogs would bolt a whole can down in two or three bites. My conclusion was that it had to be tasty, and Archie wouldn't eat it if it was inedible, so I stuck my little fingers into the can and pulled out a nice-sized appetizer.

I initially took a small taste, and it wasn't that bad even with the grainy texture, so I took another small bite. At that point Archie lost it; he could no longer keep a straight face and started laughing hysterically. I was still clueless and asked him what was so funny. He said he couldn't believe that I actually ate horse meat. My counterargument was that he did too, and it didn't taste that bad. He was rolling on the ground laughing when he said, "I didn't eat any." Terror filled my young heart as I thought, maybe it would poison me or make me sick and perhaps even kill me. Archie assured me that I would be fit as a fiddle. *Should I believe him this time, or should I ask Dad when he gets home?*

I learned a valuable lesson that day. Canned dog food is edible, and I can always resort to that if there is no human food available. Archie learned a good lesson also which was that when Dad arrived home, he would be getting a spanking. I told my mom what happened and her response to Archie was, "You just wait until your dad gets home!" That one sentence was torment to all of us kids. We hated waiting until Dad got home to receive our punishment. Just spank me already so I don't have to anticipate it all day long. Some days I would get busy playing and forget that I had a spanking coming when Dad arrived. I was always excited to see him unless there was a paddling to be delivered. When playing outside in the front yard we could see our dad's pickup truck headed our way driving down the gravel road from probably a half mile away, and someone would holler, "Here comes Daddy!" That would empty our small home as we all ran to the front yard to greet Dad. He must have felt like a billionaire with so much attention being showered upon him with hugs and kisses to boot.

We were all thrilled when Dad arrived home from work, and on most days my siblings would argue over which one of us would take off his shoes.

My mom had the memory of an elephant and never forgot when one of us had a spanking coming. Her dreaded words were, "Guess what Billy did today?" Trepidation would take hold of me as I waited for Dad to pull that thin leather belt through his belt loops then double it over and use it on my rear end. He would take my left hand into his left hand, and the dance would commence. I would run in a circle as he swatted my bottom three or four times until it was all over with but the crying. I would heal up and hair over in no time. I received oodles of spankings up until I was about eleven. I finally learned that if I didn't engage in such stupid behavior there would be no spanking or I at the very least had to be sneaky enough not to get caught. My dad always said, "I don't know why you have to spank a kid's butt to put brains in their head." The spankings have made me a genius. Dad never spanked me as often as I deserved. I was sneaky and got away with scads of unsavory behavior.

Later on that summer, Vernie, Cameron, and I decided to take my dad's bird dog, Bridgette, for a walk in the woods. We didn't like to keep the dogs cooped up in their pen all day. Our house was surrounded by oak trees, hickory trees, pecan trees and cedar trees just to name a few of the many varieties of plant life in the area. Poison ivy and poison sumac were also a common find. I am not sure how we survived running through those woods with no adult supervision. My mom was simply thrilled that we were outside and out of her hair. There were snakes galore in those woods and some were poisonous. Copperheads and the occasional rattlesnake could have been a real problem but somehow, we were never bitten. We had a pet boxer dog named Brindle that was very protective of our family. The day Brindle died she was with me in the yard and saw or smelled a copperhead lying silently in the tall grass next to me. Brindle grabbed that snake and started shaking it to death. She killed the snake but was bitten in the process. She died later that evening, and the whole family cried because she was such a faithful companion.

Anyway, the three of us were taking my dad's bird dog for a walk in the timber and it was always an adventure while in the woods. We would take off running into those woods in shorts, T-shirts, and flip-flops or PF. Flyers, and somehow, the poison ivy or poison sumac never affected me. If you encountered the oil found on the leaves of those plants, you would develop a horrible itchy bright red rash that would take weeks to heal up. I later learned that it was a good idea to wear long pants while in the timber. The three of us had walked a considerable distance from the house when Vernie decided he had to go number two. We were probably a mile from the house, and Vernie couldn't hold it long enough to make the trek back. He proceeded to drop his shorts and relieve himself right there under a big oak tree. He grabbed a hand full of leaves—to finish up the process—and as soon as he pulled up his shorts, Bridgette ran up to that oak tree and bolted down that recycled food in about two gulps. All three of us screamed and were totally grossed out by what had just occurred.

As soon as Bridgette was done with her snack, she thought it was playtime again and tried to jump up on us and lick us. The more we pushed her away, the more she thought playtime was in full swing and desperately wanted to lick our bare legs. We kept screaming, "No," and "Get away!", but to no avail. I was the youngest one present, and to this day I think I was the smartest one there. I had a plan on how I was not going to be licked by a turd-eating dog. All I had to do was outrun my brother and sister back to the house, and if I got a head start, it was very doable. While Vernie and Cameron were preoccupied with pushing the dog away from their bare legs that Bridgette desperately wanted to lick, I took off, like a scolded pup, at a dead run for the house.

Vernie and Cameron looked up and saw me high tailing it out of there and immediately comprehended the wisdom in getting as far away from that dog as possible. As I looked back, they started running after me. Poor Cameron tripped while jumping over a wild grapevine and stumbled to the ground. Bridgette still thought it was all fun and games as she licked my poor sister's face. Cameron's screams for help echoed through the woods behind me as I ran toward the house. It was every man for himself, and I was not going back. I was the first one there and stayed in the house the rest of the day, close to Mom for protection so that my older sister wouldn't abuse me. Vernie thought he had escaped unscathed...until the next morning. His butt crack started to itch and developed a red rash that made it look like an orangutan's bright red inflamed booty. He was freaked out over his insanely chafed backside and asked Mom because his bottom was all ablaze. She asked him if he had wiped with leaves while out in the woods and when he said yes, she knew what the issue was. He had wiped it with poison ivy! Mom smeared calamine lotion on his rear end for the next two weeks in an attempt to heal Vernie's painfully itchy burning crack. It always paid off big time to be smart or at least get a head start on everyone else.

5

Fastest Man Alive

I suspected that Leroy was bored one summer day when he came up with the idea of how to become the fastest man in the world. He would not attempt such a feat for himself but would somehow persuade his younger brother, Archie, to take the crown. Leroy was approximately fifteen years old at the time, and Archie was eleven. We lived six miles from the nearest city whose population was only about 600 people. Our house was isolated from the rest of the world with an abundance of woodland and some pasture, and there were no other neighbors for miles, so we were stuck with each other and whatever we could find to occupy our days. When it came to driving while in the country, age was not a consideration; if you could see over the steering wheel and reach the brake and gas pedal, you were good to go.

In 1964, my dad owned a 1951 Chevy step-side pickup truck. On the step-side trucks between the door and rear fender, there was a step used to stand on to reach into the bed of the truck. Leroy convinced Archie that he could make it possible for him to be faster than Jesse Owens, the Olympic track star. Jesse Owens ran 21.7 miles per hour, and Archie was now convinced that he could reach 22 miles per hour and claim the title. He was all ears as Leroy explained step by step how he could break the world's record and become the fastest man alive! Leroy would drive my dad's green 1951 pickup while Archie rode on the step on the outside of the truck. Once the truck reached the championship speed of 22 miles per hour, Archie would then leap from his perch and run for a short distance into the record books.

It all seemed like a piece of cake to Archie as he took up his position on the exterior of the truck. Leroy started the truck engine, and Archie hollered, "Let's go!" They headed down the gravel road in front of our house, and Archie was so proud that his big brother was doing him such a huge favor. He knew that once they hit twenty-two, he would go down in history as the fastest man alive. As the truck approached that crowning velocity, Leroy yelled from the driver's seat and told Archie to get ready to leap into the history books.

At twenty-two miles per hour, Leroy yelled, "Jump!" and Archie did not hesitate in the least. Glory was well within his grasp. He leapt from the side, glanced over into the cab and saw Leroy laughing wildly. Archie had a look of sheer desperation on his face as reality set in, and he realized he had been duped by Leroy once again. His first foot hit the gravel, and it was all he could do to plant that second foot as the top of his body began to outpace his legs. That was one giant step for mankind, and there would not be another as he toppled into the ditch and rolled end over end for quite some distance through the tall brush and weeds. When he came to rest in the vegetation, covered by a cloud of dust, he somehow survived with only minor abrasions and bruises.

Leroy was in big trouble when Dad found out. He was old enough that Dad didn't spank him, but the scolding he received for his crime beat him down just the same. Dad's harsh words were like the piercings of a sword. Surprisingly enough, my siblings are still alive, even after the outrageous and dangerous antics that we perpetrated on one another.

6

Mrs. Owen

In 1964, I began first grade at Lincoln Elementary. Leroy was a senior that year and would soon head off to college. Lincoln was a small-town school with only twelve students in my first-grade class. Mrs. Owen, my strict, no-nonsense teacher, was older than most of the other teachers. Back then there were no kids with ADD, ADHD, or any other type of condition to explain their undisciplined behavior. Spankings at school were common, and that seemed to cure ADD, ADHD, and any other conditions that today somehow require pre-scription meds. My dad was a master at spanking ADD, ADHD, or any other ailment right out of us kids.

Mrs. Owen had her hands full dealing with me. I was a rowdy, ram-bunctious five-year-old, and if I didn't receive the discipline that all kids need, I was into everything. Those were the days when teachers ruled with a rod of iron, or at least by a three-foot-long paddle with holes drilled in it for less wind resistance found in the principal's office. Believe it or not, I made it through twelve years of school with-out a single paddling. My good fortune was most likely not because of my stellar behavior but because my dad was on the school board. Teachers were smart and didn't want to spank the children of school board members who were involved in the hiring and firing of school staff. My dad more than made up for the lack of school spankings at home. If I was in trouble at school, my teacher would send a note home, and that would seal my fate.

Being one of eight siblings, I was always talking and sharing with other classmates, which did not bode well with Mrs. Owen. Her solution to shut me up when I was unruly was to pull my hair and pull it, she did. I couldn't say that I didn't have it coming, but she sure was rough on me. This went on for months, and I was growing very weary of the hair pulling. At five years old (yes, I started first grade at age five), I decided to take matters into my own hands and solve the problem. I had a foolproof solution that would provide some relief. I figured if I had my hair cut short—maybe a crew cut—that would solve my dilemma. I would be able to chitchat with my friends, and there would be absolutely no consequences. So, I talked to my dad about getting a haircut on Saturday and told him I wanted a crew cut. He was delighted! Dad was wholly against boys having long hair.

It seemed like an eternity waiting for Saturday to arrive, but I knew things were about to get much more to my liking at school. Saturday finally arrived, and Dad took me and Vernie to our local barbershop for haircuts. This was the typical barbershop of the day with the candy cane looking sign out front and the smell of men's grooming products and cigarette smoke inside. I still had to sit on that stupid booster seat inside the giant hydraulic barber chair. I couldn't wait until I was big enough to leave the booster seat to the little kids. Our barber had girlie magazines in the backroom for the men to look at. They would take a men's magazine like *Outdoor Life* or *Field & Stream* and place a *Playboy* magazine inside so that it looked as if they were reading about hunting and fishing. Hunting and fishing magazines don't have a centerfold. I was never fooled by that. Dad never participated in looking at girlie magazines, at least while I was there.

I told Murray, our barber, that I wanted a crew cut, and he grabbed his electric clippers and began removing the source of my many painful moments at school. In a matter of minutes, I was one eighth of an inch from being totally bald. After Murray dusted the hair clippings from my head and shoulders, he gave me a stick of Wrigley's Juicy Fruit chewing gum for my troubles. I felt very naked and embarrassed about my choice of hairdo. Vernie was already laughing and making fun of me until Dad put a stop to that. The teasing didn't get any better when we arrived at home. My other siblings all ganged up on me and made fun of me because of how silly I looked. This was just a foretaste of things to come at school. What had I done? Kids can be so cruel!

As my siblings got used to my bald head that weekend, they gradually stopped teasing me, and Helga decided that she needed a haircut, too. My mom always fixed my sisters' hair up real fancy like. Dad preferred that his wife and daughters have long, beautiful hair, and they certainly did. Mom had arranged Helga's hair into banana curls that hung down all around her head. Helga thought she needed a trim, and I was more than willing to try out my barbering skills on her lovely banana curls. I found Mom's scissors and cut two of those long, beautiful curls off and hid them in the desk drawer. With so many of us running around, no one even noticed my great barbering job until Mom washed and was combing out Helga's hair that evening. She asked Helga if she had cut her hair, and she was quick to say that Billy had cut off her curls. I received a spanking for what I thought was a very stylish haircut. Mom found the curls hidden in the desk drawer a few weeks later, and I had to hear for the second time how I was not allowed to cut anyone's hair again. I was afforded a few moments of peace and quiet before I returned to school on Monday.

Back at school, my friends, Orson and Frank, told me how funny I looked and really enjoyed laughing at me and teasing me about my naked head. I tried to explain why I got all of my hair cut off, and they said it sounded stupid to them. I was beginning to have doubts about my master plan. I was still standing by my decision and just knew that Mrs. Owen had finally met her match, and she would realize that a first grader had outsmarted her. The school bell rang, and everyone headed from the playground to the classroom. Anticipation was high as I thought of how Mrs. Owen would react to the fact that she could not pull my hair or stop me from visiting with my classmates.

When class got underway and the books were opened, we read about Dick, Jane, Sally, and Spot in the hopes of learning some new words. I spun around in my desk and started visiting with Frank. He kept telling me to be quiet or we would be in big trouble. I knew I had my secret weapon, which was no hair. Things were going just as planned, and first grade was looking better than ever. I continued to turn around at my desk and visit with Frank when a shadow overtook me from behind. Mrs. Owen was standing right next to my desk and glaring at me like an angry bear. I was fearless! She told me to turn around and face the front of the classroom and to stop chatting, so I turned around and looked straight up at her and smiled a mischievous grin.

I knew that she was eager to pull my hair, but guess what Mrs. Owen, NO HAIR! She stood there for a moment staring at me with that huge smile on my face. "What are you grinning about?" she peevishly asked. I was about to burst at the seams and could hardly contain myself because I knew I had won.

I couldn't hold it in any longer and blabbered that proud statement, "I got all of my hair cut off so that you can't pull it anymore!" I then leaned back on my desk and folded my arms, that celebratory smile still on my face, knowing it was a victorious day for students everywhere. Without warning, Mrs. Owen grabbed my right ear, and I could have sworn she was striving to remove it! I let out a screech that got the attention of the whole classroom. She told me that if I didn't turn around and stop chatting, she was going to remove that ear, and if that didn't work, then she would remove the other ear also. Wow, I never saw that coming and obviously didn't think my master plan all the way through. I was okay with the hair, but I really needed my ears, and losing them was not an option. When I got older and needed glasses, how would they stay on my face without ears? People would really make fun of me with no ears.

Teachers are way more resourceful than we give them credit. Mrs. Owen checkmated me in one smart move. She not only taught me the three Rs—reading, writing, arithmetic—but many valuable life lessons. She taught me to respect people in places of authority which many of today's youth don't possess. She also taught me that when we misbehave, there are always unavoidable consequences. It was mercy that left my ears intact.

Mrs. Owen was diagnosed with cancer about midway through my first-grade year. She died in late spring. Her funeral was the first that I attended, and I can still remember struggling to see over the side of the open casket to say one last good-bye to a great teacher. I have often wondered if she ever realized what a positive influence she had on my young life. Everyone reading this book has a teacher to thank for that ability and for a thousand other skills that make life much more delightful and fulfilling.

After Mrs. Owen died, I realized for the first time that people die and that I would one day die. That had a profound impact on my life. I began asking my mom if orange juice or any number of other things would kill me. Mom was very comforting and assured me that I would live for a very long time. She was right because moms just know that sort of stuff.

7

Benton's Ford Bridge

To get to our itty-bitty cottage in the woods, you had to cross the Whitetail River at a location known as Benton's Ford. At that location there was a wooden swinging bridge suspended by large steel cables. It spanned the entire width of the river. The bridge had been there a long time and had been repaired on numerous occasions. During repairs in 1940, the bridge completely collapsed, killing six people— of which two were just spectators. A replacement bridge was built in the same location and was equally as scary as the original, with the wooden floor of the bridge creaking and groaning under the weight of cars and trucks.

I was in second grade in the fall of 1965 when the state condemned the bridge. Our short school bus was not allowed to drive over the bridge while loaded with students. Even though there were only about a dozen students on the bus, we were expected to unload on one side of the bridge, walk across and wait for the bus to drive across empty, and then we would all pile back in. The bridge was suspended about fifty feet above the river, and on a windy day, that creaky wooden structure would bounce up and down in the breeze. There were always boards missing and you could see straight through to the rushing water below. Crossing the river at a different location would have taken at least an hour longer, and the school district had decided that unloading and reloading the bus at each end of the bridge was the route to go.

I still can't believe they allowed young children like me and my siblings to walk across that death trap. Several of the platform boards were missing, and others were curled up on the ends, which made for plenty of tripping hazards. I remember walking on the 2x12s that ran lengthways and hoping and praying I wouldn't stumble and fall through one of the many holes where planks were missing. There were so many boards missing in some areas that several kids could fall into the fast-moving water and be lost forever. None of us knew how to swim, which made this even more unnerving. I have had countless nightmares over the years about this river and walking across that death trap of a bridge. Things were certainly different in the 1960s.

Wintertime 1965, I was attending second grade, and Mrs. Smith was my teacher. Half of the classroom was for second grade, and third grade sat on the other side of the room. Mrs. Smith taught both classes, and I was sure she did not get double pay. There were twelve students in my second-grade class and about that many in the third grade. Mrs. Smith would start out by getting the second grade busy on assignments and then move to the other side of the room and teach the third graders. She would switch back and forth throughout the day.

At the end of one school day, a day that will live in infamy, Mrs. Smith was finishing up lessons on the third-grade side of the room. I raised my hand to get permission to go to the restroom. A gurgling in my bowels intensified with every passing moment. Very disturbing. Pressure was building, and it seemed that Mrs. Smith couldn't have cared less about my desperate plight. I knew she could see me frantically waving my hand, but she chose to ignore me and continued instructing the third graders. If she had known that I was about to explode, she would have given me the green light, but there I painfully sat. I did not want to do a number two at school but would have to make an exception this time.

When I was in first grade, while using the toilet at school, a couple of high school boys came into the restroom and made fun of me. There were no doors on the stalls, so I was in plain view. They called me turd boy, threw wet paper towels at me, and laughed as they exited the restroom. All I could do was hang my head down in shame until they departed. It was a very humbling experience and not one that I cared to repeat but, when you got to go, you got to go.

Mrs. Smith was busy teaching the other class, and it was clear that she didn't have time for me or my impending disaster. I held my hand up several times, and she continued to overlook me. My bowels had expanded to the max by this time, and I felt like I would burst from the mounting pressure. I considered standing up and running to the restroom without permission but knew that was a death sentence. In the 1960s, teachers put up with no nonsense, and I did not want both of my ears removed as punishment. I continued to hold on, hoping that the bell would ring, and I could race to the commode for some relief. I fought the high-pressure as long as I could, but it was just too much. "OH NO!" I filled my pants with a burst of foam. What have I done? How will I conceal this? I would be the butt of everyone's jokes, and I couldn't let it get out that I had pooped my pants at school! I would never live this down if the other kids found out.

After exploding, I stopped raising my hand and laid my head on my desk, entirely humiliated and embarrassed. I did not cry, but I for sure wanted to. Before the bell rang, Mrs. Smith would call on each row of students to go to the back of the classroom and retrieve their coats. Row one wraps, row two wraps and so on until we all regained our coats. Good thing for me it was winter, and I had on a long coat to cover my derriere and hide the brown seeping into my jeans. After putting on my coat and feeling somewhat concealed, the pressure continued to build again, and I had another discharge before the bell rang to dismiss us for the day. At that point the restroom was no good to me. I needed to be taken to a carwash for high-pressure cleaning. My tighty-whiteys were rapidly reaching maximum capacity. Finally, we were dismissed to our respective buses.

Our school bus was more of a van and only held a dozen students. Don, the only senior on the bus, always sat in the front passenger seat next to the bus driver who was always eating peppermint candies. Our bus driver was an older man, and he kept that bag of peppermints hidden in his coat pocket and periodically reached in and snuck one into his mouth. Don rode up front every day because he was the oldest student on board. I was hoping for the backseat this day, for obvious reasons, but by the time I arrived at the bus, the only seat left was on the console facing the back, between the driver and Don. I was still trying to hide my misfortune and thought I had done a pretty good job up to that point. As I took my seat, a warm sensation crept up the lower part of my back. My undies had filled to maximum capacity and were overflowing! Things were very serious at that point, and I wondered how long before the smell would permeate the entire bus. I was miserable at that juncture and trying to keep this a secret was more and more difficult.

After a few stops, a seat was available in the back of the bus, and I hurried back there to take advantage of my imagined seclusion. Once seated, I had to go again. Ugh! I was still thankful for my big coat—my only hope of keeping my dreadful mess quiet. After another stop, it was now time to cross the river. As I mentioned earlier, all the students on the bus had to walk across Benton's Ford Bridge, and the bus would pick us up on the other side. The only students left on the bus were my five siblings and Don. That was the most unpleasant walk I had ever taken in my life. I was scared to death of falling through that bridge and drowning in the freezing cold water below. It was bone-chilling and frightening on that old rickety bridge, and my pants were now filled and overflowing with icy cold foam. What was once warm in my shorts was now cold, wet, and very smelly. Could things get any worse? Getting back on the bus was no better. I scurried to my seat in the back and hung my head in disgrace. I just wanted to get home and get cleaned up.

Just when I thought things couldn't get any worse, Don piped up and said, "It smells like somebody has been skinning coyotes!" My siblings laughed, and I assumed they all thought someone had passed gas. Somehow no one discovered the extent of my ordeal. We at long last arrived at the front door of our minuscule home, and I was determined to get inside and clean myself up before anyone discovered my misery.

As we walked through the front door, Mom greeted us and knew by the look on my face that something was awry. Moms are very intuitive. I just hung my head in shame as she approached me, and the stench overwhelmed her. "What is that smell?" she apprehensively asked. At that point I totally broke down and cried. I told her that Mrs. Smith would not let me go to the restroom, and I just couldn't hold it any longer. Mom stripped me down and gasped when she saw the horrid mess hiding in my jeans. She put me in our small metal shower because I was covered front and back with awfulness. I must have been dreaming to imagine that I could get cleaned up on my own without anyone finding out. When my dad arrived home from work that day and my mom told him what had happened, he was furious. He called Mrs. Smith on the phone that evening, and I realized that my dad was not afraid of her. He told her in no uncertain terms this had better never happen again. Dad also told me, "If you must use the restroom and a teacher won't acknowledge you, just get up and go to the restroom anyway. If they don't like it, they can call me." Anyone who knew my dad understood that you did not want to be on his bad side. For some reason, my siblings didn't rat me out at school, and I can only assume it was because Dad had threatened them with their life if they told anyone; after all, I was his baby boy. Dad had his flaws, but he always had your back.

8

Animal Control

Living in the country in the 1960s was sure different from 2022. We had dogs and cats galore, all of which lived outside. We couldn't squeeze anyone else into our tiny home. It was amazing how many dogs and cats were produced when their population growth went unchecked. Cats were always having kittens, and the dogs were having loads of puppies. Spay and neuter were not words in our vocabulary. I found out early on that the animal kingdom takes care of the population growth itself, but only to a certain extent.

I remember one spring day when a momma cat had a litter of kittens in our old smokehouse, which was decades ago used as a place to smoke meat and was now just a shed in which to store lots of junk. The smokehouse was positioned behind our house, and the momma cat had hidden her kittens in there. All of us loved those fluffy little balls of fur and were overjoyed when we happened upon a new litter of kittens. That particular litter produced five kittens that were newly born with their eyes still unopened. At around eight to ten days old, their eyes would slowly begin to open. All kittens are born with blue eyes, and as they age, they change to their adult eye color. Those new kittens were so tiny and cute to view and caress. For several days, we looked forward to visiting the smokehouse to see how the little baby kitties were doing.

One morning, Helga and I were headed to the shed to get our daily dose of kittens. We were shocked and appalled by what we found. The only thing left of our furry little creatures was a bunch of kitten heads scattered about on the floor of the shed. Kitten heads were everywhere! I was only five years old, and Helga was four. We couldn't believe our eyes. What in the world had killed the newest furry additions to our family? Dad would know what happened, so I waited for him to arrive home from work. He showed up later that afternoon, and I told him about the kitten heads in the smokehouse. His conclusion was that the momma cat hid her kittens so the tom cats couldn't find them. Tom cats will kill and eat all kittens that they did not sire. It all sounded reasonable to a five-year-old, and of course my dad knew about everything.

When you live in the country where there are hordes of animals, you learn where babies come from. I had seen puppies born and kittens born and even some horses and cattle at some of the local farms.

One summer day, Vernie and I were playing ball in the tall grass next to our house. He stepped backward and accidentally stepped on a cat that was very pregnant. When he stepped on her, a kitten popped out of her. We both yelled, "Yuck!" The kitten had afterbirth all over it and the momma cat started licking her kitten and cleaning it up. In no time, she got up and carried her clean newborn baby to a hiding place and gave birth to three more with no complications. I concluded that it did little or no damage to her when Vernie stepped on her. Somehow our cat population was kept in check. I don't think it was the tom cats that should get the credit. I am assuming that the same way our dog population was regulated involved cat control also.

Throughout the year, we were also blessed with litters of puppies, and I soon learned who was in charge of animal control in our neck of the woods. Several times, I accompanied my father on a trip to Benton's Ford Bridge. Before heading to the river, we would round up the newborn puppies. Dad would place a concrete block in the bottom of a burlap sack and place all the puppies inside of the bag. He would then tie a string around the top of the bag and put the bag into the bed of the pickup. Off we would go, headed for Benton's Ford Bridge. Dad would drive to the middle of the bridge, park, and look both ways to make sure that no one was within sight. He would then get out of the truck and grasp the sack of puppies and drop them over the side of the bridge into the river below. All the puppies yelped as they dropped into the fast-moving water. The bag sank quickly because of the concrete block in the bottom. There was no more yelping; only bubbles could be seen as the bag drifted with the current downstream. My heart also sank! Dad said he had to do it because we could not afford to feed that many dogs, and no one else would take them. His reasoning made it no less painful to observe. Through the years, late at night in my dreams, I often heard those hopeless whimpers from the puppies falling into the river. I would awake with tears streaming down my cheeks from a heart overflowing with sorrow.

9

Paybacks

I don't believe Vernie cared much for me at all. He was always so cruel to me. He was older by three and a half years and older than three of my sisters. We all received an unsavory portion of his wrath. It consistently felt as though I was administered a double portion. I assumed he was jealous of me because Dad and I got along so well.

Many times, Dad desired my assistance on some project that I honestly did not want to participate in, but I helped him despite that. I had a good work ethic, and Vernie was on the lazy side. He didn't want to help Dad, and in turn, Dad got to the point where he didn't want his help either. Vernie didn't like how our father often referred to me as his baby boy, and it was used as a term of endearment. He wanted a moniker of his own and would sarcastically refer to me as *baby boy*. Their relationship did not improve over the years as mine did with Dad, considering I had spent so much one-on-one time with him. Vernie showed no interest in our father, and I never understood why. Looking back, I regret not having spent more time with both of my parents.

Vernie became so mad at me during one encounter that he threw me down on the floor and sat on my stomach while choking me with both of his hands around my neck. I still think his goal was to kill me, and when I did in fact, pass out, he figured his task was complete. When I regained consciousness, he was nowhere to be found. I presumed he had left me for dead. He later wished he had killed me because I told Mom and when Dad got home, it was time to put brains into Vernie's head once again.

Another time, when my dad was not home and my mom had prepared our dinner, I must have said or done something to infuriate Vernie. I was seated at the dinner table with a full plate of food, which included hot mashed potatoes and gravy. He strolled up behind my chair and forced my face directly into the hot food then exited the kitchen. I screamed and hollered, and my mom told him that he was going to get it when Dad got home from work. It seemed to me Vernie was always looking for ways to make my existence intolerable.

At a different juncture, Helga was fed up with his mistreatment and locked him out of the house. She stood at the back door, making faces at Vernie and laughing at him through the large pane of glass in the upper half. Helga had bested him, and she loved it. Vernie instructed her several times to unlock the door or else. She continued to laugh and stuck her face against the glass with her tongue poked out at him. She was really letting him have it until he punched his fist through that pane of glass and into her face. Helga started screaming that she had glass in her eyes, and Vernie was not the least bit concerned. There was no glass in her eyes, and Vernie received only a few minor cuts from the incident. When Dad came home that day, Vernie was richly rewarded with Dad's thin leather belt across his butt. Dad knew how to bring balance back to the universe with that painful leather belt.

On yet another summer day, several of us were playing outside and ended up at the small farm pond that was a short walk from our house. Everything was going fine until I did something that upset Vernie. Just existing seemed to make me a potential target. We were standing at the edge of the pond when he decided that he would push me into the water in an attempt to drown me. I was only six and had no idea how to swim, nor did he. When I fell into the water, I started hollering and thrashing about and soon realized that all I had to do was stand up. The water was shallow where he pushed me in, and I survived yet another one of his attempts to get rid of me. I ran back to the house, soaking wet and crying all the way. I told my mom what he had done to me. When he finally came back to the house, Mom told him, "You just wait until your dad gets home!"

Waiting for a spanking was torture. I always wanted to just get my spankings over with and get back to playing. Now for Vernie, I didn't mind if he had to wait and anticipate that thin leather belt across his rear end. He was somewhat off the hook until Dad arrived home, so later that afternoon, we all decided to play in and around a large oak tree growing next to the gravel road that passed by our house. I thoroughly enjoyed climbing trees. There were bird nests to check out, and if the tree was tall enough, you could see for miles in all directions. That large oak tree had a limb about ten or twelve feet above the ground that grew straight out from the trunk and extended over the gravel road. It was a perfect limb for a swing but would place the swing over the gravel road which was not practical.

Vernie thought it would be fun to crawl out on that limb and hang down by his arms. It was a neat idea and looked cool as he hung there, so proud of himself. But there was one problem. He didn't take into consideration his weak upper body strength. He did not possess the strength to pull himself back up. That limb was ten feet above the gravel road. When he realized his misfortune, he begged me and Cameron to run to the house and get a ladder. Falling on that hard gravel road below was not an option he was considering. Cameron and I both stood there looking up at him with no intention of helping him down. You see, he was also cruel to Cameron, and had attempted to drown me earlier that day. We were in no hurry to assist him, and as his cries became more desperate, he commenced to threaten us.

Cameron and I looked at each other and smiled as Vernie grew weaker and weaker and more hopeless with each passing moment. His menacing threats did not dissuade us the least bit. We were determined to see his payback for the many abusive things he had said and done to each of us. So, we watched and waited. He didn't hang there near long enough for my liking, and when he did finally drop to the ground, he hit so hard that it knocked the wind out of him. Cameron and I ran back to the house and left him there, lying in the middle of that gravel road. We stayed in the house next to Mom for protection all that afternoon until Dad came home from work. Mom told Dad about Vernie pushing me into the pond. With sore ankles, Vernie was now going to have a sore butt too. Some days just end better than others, and this one ended great. Listening to your confrontational older brother scream while Dad put brains in his head yet again was very rewarding.

10

Mountains of Laundry

My mother was a stay-at-home mom with little or no time to spend on herself. She was tireless when it came to serving others! My father was a construction manager and worked full time. He always had time for hunting and fishing or whatever else he wanted to do. Mom was on call night and day, and she had a servant's heart, and everyone knew it.

The laundry of our family was a daunting task for her. She washed clothes for nine people. Cooking, cleaning, laundry, and a thousand other tasks filled her daily chores. I have the greatest love and respect for my mom and for the wonderful parent that she was. She seemed to never get any free time for herself, and what time was available to her was typically interrupted by one of us kids. Our wee little house had no washer and dryer for years while living there. I do remember my mother using the old ringer type washer in the front yard when the weather was warm enough. The work involved with that old washing machine was, I guess, better than washing clothes at the creek using a washboard.

That old house had a water cistern. There was no water well, so we had to haul water to fill the cistern. Water was a precious commodity at our place, and Dad was always yelling about not wasting it.

I had to take showers with two of my older brothers in order to conserve water. My oldest brother was allowed to shower by himself because a three-foot-by-three-foot shower wouldn't accommodate all four of us.

Most of the time, the endless baskets of dirty laundry were loaded up in the back of our 1958 Pontiac station wagon and taken into the small town nearby that had a laundromat. There were several occasions when I was forced to wear somewhat dirty clothes to school because the laundry had not been done for the week. My clothes were likely the most difficult to get clean because I would use my shirt sleeves for a napkin, and playing outside was similar to mud wrestling. To this day, I can't keep a shirt clean through some sort of dribbling! I guess some habits never die.

One morning before school, I informed my mom that I didn't have any clean underwear. Her solution was for me to wear a pair of Cameron's panties. That sent a frightful lightning bolt through me that would last for years. I was not sure if Mom was just teasing me or serious, but there was no way I was wearing Cameron's panties, no matter how soft and pretty they were! Death was a much more reasonable solution than that. Mom would not let me attend school commando, so I wore a slightly used pair of my own tighty-whities. I had nightmares for years about being at school with nothing on but Cameron's panties, and of course my friend, Frank, was laughing hysterically and pointing me out to the whole school. What might seem inconsequential to Mom could be terrifying to a six-year-old.

On another weekday, we had a school concert, and Mom was bringing my dress clothes to change into at school. I was going to switch clothes in the boys' restroom, but Mom didn't think that I could handle it by myself. Her solution was to help me change clothes in the *girls'* restroom. I was not having any part of that! Her Plan C was to undress me and redress me right there in the hallway between the restrooms in plain sight. Mom won, and that's what we did. Before I knew it, she had me stripped down to my tighty-whiteys in the hallway as several of the girls in my class walked by giggling. I was humiliated! Mom did whatever it took to get her motherly job done, and most of the time it was just fine. I was so thankful that I was wearing my own underwear that day and they were clean.

11

Bedwetting Champion

I cannot—nor would I desire to—claim the title "Bedwetting Champion" of my family. That title goes to my oldest brother, Leroy. He was fourteen years old the last time he christened his sheets. I do, however, accept the silver medal seeing that I was twelve when I had my last mishap. As if my poor mother didn't have enough on her plate, she had extra laundry to clean because of my brother and me. Bedwetting was yet another one of those family secrets you didn't want the kids at school to find out about. They would have teased me relentlessly, so I did what I could to keep this information from leaving our home.

I had accidents several nights per week up until I was about eight or nine years old. The frequency dropped to once per week after receiving some helpful recommendations. The best advice I ever received about bedwetting was from my aunt Clara. She informed me that I needed to stretch out my bladder so it would hold more, and I wouldn't have those mishaps. I presumed that she meant I should hold it and wait, if I could, before going. She also instructed me not to drink an abundance of liquids right before bed and especially no soda pop prior to bed. My bladder must have been the size of a pea because I was going all the time as a kid. Living in the great outdoors provided a restroom at every turn. My sisters generally found the toilet option preferable, for obvious reasons, but not when nature was screaming their name. Aunt Clara's advice seemed to work in lieu of the fact that I went from several nights per week to maybe one accident each week. Occasionally was better than every other night.

Bedwetting had a huge impact on my social life during my childhood. I desperately wanted to be a boy scout, but overnight campouts were not something I was willing to risk. I never slept over at a friend's house for the same reason. My other siblings often spent the night with friends, but not me. I was destined to be a stay-at-home bedwetter.

When I was twelve years old, my dad signed me up to attend a baseball camp that was in the central part of our state. It was about a three-hour drive to get there. Baseball camp was supposed to last seven days, and I would learn the basics of playing baseball. It all sounded great to me because there was also swimming, hiking, fishing, and none of my siblings. Children from big families often wish they were an only child, and the only child dreams of having lots of siblings to play with. Go figure! My bedwetting had been kept in check for several months with no soaked sheets, so I was primed and willing for a week with no brothers or sisters. I felt ever so special when my dad purchased a wooden footlocker to place at the end of my bed in the barracks. I treasured that footlocker because it was a surprise gift from Dad, and I was the only one in my family who possessed one. Things were sure looking up that summer.

At long last, the time finally came to head to camp and enjoy a week of me-time with fun stuff to do every day. Dad and I arrived at camp, and he helped me get everything unloaded and into the barracks before he took off for home. I was heavyhearted as he drove off and left me there all alone. I realized that I was on my own. I had never gone anywhere by myself for an entire week. It was all so new to me. There were plenty of other boys from twelve to sixteen years old. Some were just plain mean like my brother, Vernie. You just can't get away from that sort of person. I quickly figured out who to hang with and who to avoid. The older boys relished getting into towel fights in the barracks. They would roll up their bath towel in such a manner that it was big on one end and tiny on the other. They called them rat tails because of their shape, and they were used against one another like bullwhips. If utilized correctly, and the small end was wet, they would snap loudly when they struck something. The older boys waged war with those rat tails and would produce bruises on the backs, legs, and arms of their opponents. It all appeared far too painful for me to join in, plus, being a small twelve-year-old, they wanted nothing to do with me.

The week was absolutely flying by. My time at camp was scheduled with batting practice, pitching lessons, and fielding classes each day. My free time was spent in the swimming pool or hiking in the surrounding woods. Watching the rat tail fights—from a safe distance—was entertaining. If you ventured too close though, you were a target for their whips.

I was so proud of myself; it was the last night of camp, and my bed sheets were still dry as a bone. It was Saturday night and time to enjoy our last night in the wilderness party. We had a huge bonfire, big logs to sit on around the blazing flames of the campfire, and plenty of hotdogs to roast, along with chips, s'mores, and soda pop. I was having the time of my life! It had been an amazing week. Everybody went to bed at lights out, which was at ten o'clock. Each barracks had an adult on watch to keep the peace and to ensure that things went as scheduled.

I slept like a fat baby that night and dreamed that I hit the game-winning home run in the World Series. I was in such a deep sleep that I also envisioned myself entering the restroom at the baseball stadium and began to use the urinal. Oh, what a sweet relief. In the past, I had oftentimes dreamed that I was in the bathroom relieving myself and would wake up in a panic, realizing that I had wet the bed. It was 5:30 on the a.m. side of Sunday morning at baseball camp, and I had just wet the bed! *NOOOOOOOOOO!* It must have been those Pepsi Colas I drank at the bonfire. I had broken one of the cardinal rules for dry sheets and I knew I was going to pay dearly for it. What had I done? I would be the laughingstock of the camp and did not want to be referred to as pee-pee boy or Billy wet-wet as my siblings so lovingly referred to me. Thankfully, it was still dark at 5:30 in the morning, and no one was up or even stirring around in their beds.

The bunkbeds that we slept on were lined up on each side of the barracks with about three feet of walking space between beds. I had to be stealthy to hide the incriminating evidence. The first thing I did was remove the bedding and stash it in the footlocker at the end of my bunk. For obvious reasons, I was pleased that I had been placed in a bottom bunk. Each camper brought their own bedding from home, so it was no problem to sneak the wet sheets out of the barracks and hopefully only my laundry lady, Mom, would be the wiser. That solved one problem. Now there was this huge wet spot on the mattress that I had to conceal. And conceal it I did. My next genius move was to quietly flip the mattress over, and it worked like a charm. The urine did not soak all the way through the mattress, which left one side dry, and that was all I needed.

After flipping the mattress over, I thought of the next guy that would sleep in that bunk. Poor sucker! Would everyone think that he wet the bed? Would there be a lingering odor after my departure?

What torment and ridicule would he have to endure? Oh well, better him than me.

Once I had concealed all the incriminating evidence, it was then time to shower. I figured out years ago that a skunk does not think he stinks even though he reeks. If you don't bathe after wetting the bed, you will stink, and others will notice. There was a girl in my class at school who always smelled of urine, and everyone talked about it behind her back. We figured she must be one of those bedwetters. I don't believe she showered before school as I did. I knew the smell was a dead giveaway, so I headed to the shower before anyone else woke up.

My plan worked great from start to good-smelling finish. It was now about six o'clock, and I was ready to get all my camp gear together and go enjoy breakfast in the mess hall. Dad was to arrive at ten o'clock, and believe it or not, I missed my family. As I was leaving the barracks, I could hear one of the other guys say that they could smell pee! I was out the door in a flash and never heard another word about it. For twelve years I was a bedwetter, and that was the last time I wet the bed, or at least the last time I'm willing to admit.

Here are some simple rules for all of you current bedwetters:

1. Never spend the night with a friend, for obvious reasons. If your friend can keep it a secret, then, spend the night. Discreetly wear a Depend under your pajama bottoms just in case you have an accident.

2. Never drink soda or sugary drinks before bed, especially ones with caffeine.

3. Limit your liquid intake around two hours
   prior to bed.

4. Never, never, never admit guilt, even though your
   siblings might out you to others.

5. When you do have an accident, always bathe before
   entering the public domain. Skunks don't think
   they stink either.

6. The bedwetter should never sleep on the top bunk.
   I never did. Liquid flows down.

To all the parents of bedwetters, we can't help it. Please don't make us feel worse than we already do. My parents were understanding yet frustrated with it. Kids can be vicious and some of my siblings were not so nice about it.

Share these rules with your bedwetter, and they will be forever grateful to you!

12

Two Front Teeth

How would I describe my younger sister, Helga? Well, as a child, she was always the individual crying in our family photos. Every summer, my mother would coerce us to get all dressed up for picture taking on what routinely felt like the hottest day of the year. She would compel us to stand, for what seemed like an eternity, in front of her many flower beds that had been sown with a multiplicity of colorful flowers. Mom was incredibly proud of her numerous budding rose bushes. She snapped hundreds of pictures over the years with her Kodak Brownie Camera while we posed in front of those countless blossoms. The Kodak Brownie was a camera that you held waist high and peered into the view finder on the top of the camera and then snapped the picture.

Helga was inevitably the last one dressed for pictures and enjoyed the thought of everyone waiting for her. When my mom would force her to stand next to us for the picture, she would throw a temper tantrum almost every time. She was such a brat! The rest of us just wanted it over with and back to playing, so because of Helga, it always took much longer than necessary. She and Vernie were not well liked by the rest of us because of the way they carried on all the time.

Our summer photo shoots also included snapshots of us lounging in and around our small wading pool. We got a kick out of it even though it was only twelve inches deep and about four-foot-by-four-foot square. Summer months were oppressively hot, and we had no air conditioning in our home. Splashing around in that little pool was a welcome relief from the heat. It took very little to keep us entertained while dwelling in the boondocks. My sisters wore rubber swimming caps in the pool, and I was never sure why. It was something women and girls wore back in the day. My sisters thought they were Esther Williams while donning those caps. After ten minutes of pool time, the water was so full of grass clippings and dirt from jumping in and out that we had to empty the water and refill it with fresh clean water. Helga and Vernie were a dark cloud over pool time. Helga whined and complained incessantly, while Vernie thrived on shoving me out of the pool when Mom wasn't watching. The two of them most likely peed in our pool! Oh, to be an only child.

At other times, I would be seated on the couch in our living room, and Helga would walk up behind me, snap her fingers in my ears, and taunt me. "I'm not touching you." She was starved for attention! I would ultimately grow weary of the fingers snapping next to my ears and retaliate with what I thought was a reasonable amount of pain for her annoying behavior. She would dash off to tell Mom or Dad, and my only defense was that she started it. That excuse never flew with Dad, and I would receive a spanking. Helga often peeked around the corner and watched with sinister delight as Dad paddled me. She has never outgrown that behavior and continues to stir up trouble wherever she goes.

With eight children in the family, there was bound to be more than one middle child who felt cheated in every way. Our family had two of them, Vernie and Helga. Helga was the female version of Vernie.

Both were bitter about life and most of the people in it. Vernie and Helga were both tattletales. Even as adults, they have blabbed negative things about the rest of us to our parents to get some much-desired attention—an attempt to make themselves look better. There are those moments when the universe rights a whole pile of wrongs in one fell swoop.

One thunderstorm-filled evening in May, my family was traveling home from a school function in our 1958 Pontiac station wagon. With so many of us, we always had a car full. No seat belts were required back then. My dad was driving as we pulled up and parked in front of our house. It was pouring down rain and had been for quite some time. Our patchy dirt yard was saturated and muddy. The area leading to the front door was directly through this wet, muddy path. Dad instructed us with a firm tone, "Do not run. Everybody must walk to the house!"

As soon as the backdoor of the station wagon opened, Helga took off at a full sprint for the front porch. She never listened to sound advice, and often, it got her into some painful situations. A few feet from the front porch, she slipped in a mud puddle and fell face first into the raised edge of the concrete porch. The rest of us remained in the car and watched in horror as she all but knocked out her two front teeth when attempting to take a bite out of that slab of concrete. Then we had to listen to Dad tell all of us again, "Do not run," and we could clearly see why. Those of us still in the car made our way to the front porch and caught a good look at Helga's bloody mouth. She was crying uncontrollably with a mouth full of blood drooling all over the porch.

Dad said to her, "I told you not to run!" He always liked to get that, "I told you so," in to let us know that he was right again. Helga's two front teeth were folded back in her mouth but still attached. I was only six years old and did not like witnessing all of this blood and gore. Mom pushed those two front teeth back into place while Helga screamed and sprayed blood all over Mom's clothes. The teeth remained in her mouth a few more weeks but eventually fell out. Fortunately for Helga, they were baby teeth and would have fallen out anyway. Helga has always been her own worst enemy and, to this day, scatters misery in her wake for those unlucky enough to be nearby.

13

Club Members Only

While living in the middle of nowhere, we didn't see extended family members all that often. When we did see aunts, uncles, and cousins, it was always a delight. They would typically stay for the weekend, and somehow, we made room for our guests in our petite home. On one such weekend, my cousin, Marty, was visiting, and we enjoyed the novelty of an overnight guest. Marty was the same age as Archie, and they were the oldest kids present because Leroy was now in college.

We all looked up to Archie who was somewhat feared and revered as possessing special powers. He had convinced us younger kids that he could place a curse on us. During one such incident, he rubbed a dirty stick from an oak tree on my tongue and told me that my tongue would fall off when I reached the age of sixteen. That was a huge concern of mine for years. I agonized over losing my tongue, and Archie reminded me of that curse time and again. When I finally wised up enough to realize that he had no special powers, my anxiety level was reduced considerably. He had Helga convinced that a common cottonweed, which grew wild everywhere near our residence, would give her a rash worse than poison ivy. He renamed them Rhoda Weeds. Archie would chase Helga with those large, heart-shaped leaves while chanting, "Rhoda, Rhoda, Rhoda." The name came from the 1956 movie entitled *The Bad Seed* about an evil little girl named Rhoda. Archie chased her while she screamed hysterically and the rest of us joined in the chant.

To this day, as an adult, Helga is still afraid of Rhoda Weeds and convinced they will produce a horrible rash wherever they touch her skin. I hid a Rhoda Weed in my wallet on the off chance I might bump into her.

Archie also convinced our baby sister, Monica, that she was adopted. My parents had a family portrait made about a year after Helga was born whereas they thought she was the end of the line. The picture—Monica not included—hung on our living room wall. Mom had Monica at age forty, and she was not a planned birth. I am pretty sure most of us were not planned births. Archie told Monica that she wasn't in the family photo because she was adopted, and she believed him. That teasing caused tears to well up in her big brown eyes.

To make matters worse, Archie packed a little suitcase and placed some of Monica's clothes in it and then told her the people from the orphanage were stopping by that day, and she would have to leave with them. More tears streamed from Monica's eyes. He didn't stop there; he would recruit one of us younger kids to sneak outside and knock on the front door. At that point, he informed Monica to get her suitcase because the people from the orphanage were at the front door to take her away. This went on while all of us kids would sing, "Monica, go home. Monica, go home, you are adopted, and we don't like you." Buckets of tears flowed from poor Monica. Children can be so hurtful. Monica would hide in the back of the house until Mom realized what Archie was up to and told him, "You wait until your dad gets home." Monica was the baby of the family and Dad's precious "Sweetie Pie." He was really going to get it for picking on Dad's sweetie pie. He was the only one of us kids with red hair, and we assumed that was what made him so ornery.

Archie could also make it thunder on command, or so we thought. Mom told us that thunder was made by someone dumping a wheelbarrow load of potatoes on the floor in heaven. That sounded reasonable enough to us because the people in heaven had to eat too. Archie had learned in science class that thunder is heard shortly after you see lightning. He could time it almost exactly so that when he held his arms up in the air and yelled, "Thunder!" it would thunder and scare the living daylights out of us younger kids. We figured he was in cahoots with the Devil because of that red hair. He also informed Monica that the airplane flying overhead was going to get her, and she'd become so frightened that she would run to the house crying whenever she heard an airplane overhead.

Jumping back to Marty's visit. My cousin, Marty, was spending the weekend with us, and he and Archie started their own private club that I desperately wanted to be a member of. Archie and Marty were charter members, so they weren't required to go through any kind of initiation like the rest of us. The two of them told us that new members would be allowed to hang out with them all weekend and that protection would be afforded against harassment from other siblings, aka Vernie. They discussed the initiation process with us and debated about whether to have a foot race or bike race or even push-ups or pull-ups. Archie piped up and gleefully suggested, "How about they just lick our feet, and they can be in the club?" Marty smiled an impish grin and said, "That sounds great to me." It was settled. To be in the club, we would have to lick Archie's and Marty's feet. Vernie, three years younger than them, said he would never lick their feet and did not want to be a member of their stupid club.

After hearing those words, I was even more determined to sign up. Vernie was a no go, and at that point, I would have chewed on their toenails to gain acceptance! Marty and Archie, while grinning from ear to ear, pulled off their shoes and said whoever wanted in had to lick both feet of each charter member. I don't believe they thought any of us would lick their feet as they elevated their smelly dogs. Dogs that were profusely barking. If Vernie wasn't going to be in the club, then I didn't care what I had to do to gain membership. I was the first to lick all four of their feet! It was a far cry better than eating canned dog food. I would now be protected from Vernie all weekend. Having my very own security squad for two days was well worth the price.

Cameron and Helga also licked their feet for the same reason. Vernie couldn't lay a finger on any of us all weekend because Archie told him if he did, he would be pounded into submission. It was now five against one, and Vernie did not like those numbers one iota. We teased Vernie relentlessly that weekend, and his often-repeated phrase to me was, "Just wait until Archie isn't around."

Our club decided to climb on top of the tin roof of the chicken house. We lined up along the peak of the roof and peered over at Vernie who was down on the ground on the opposite side of the building. He couldn't climb up there because he was not in the club and not allowed to fraternize with club members because Archie wouldn't allow it. We all laughed at him and repeatedly teased him. I had never had the upper hand on Vernie before, and it gave me a feeling of exuberance. The chicken house was the pen for my dad's bird dogs.

Several square, flat pieces of metal littered the ground next to the chicken house. Those were dog food cans that had been stomped flat and left lying next to the dog pen. The flat, steel pieces were about four inches by four inches in size with sharp corners. Vernie picked up several and flung them at us. We all ducked down on the back side of the tin roof so as not to get whacked by a sharp, flat piece of metal skipping off the tin and clobbering us in the face. I made the mistake of peering over the peak of that tin roof about the same time Vernie skipped one of those steel frisbees off the roof and directly into my forehead. That sent me rolling off the back side of the roof, and I smacked the ground like a gunny sack full of potatoes. I must have been part cat and had nine lives because I survived yet another painful encounter with my older brother. Vernie was very pleased with his lucky shot until Archie chased him down and twisted his arm behind his back for wounding a club member. I was permitted to stand and watch, which somehow made my wound less painful as Vernie was forced to cry out uncle. Marty's parents arrived later that afternoon and took him home. I always had this feeling of loss when our weekend guests departed. It is possible to experience a sense of loneliness even while surrounded by plenty of other people.

Monday afternoon rolled around, and Archie had baseball practice in town. That left me at home without protection from Charles Manson (Vernie) and no bodyguard. I paid for my indiscretions that day when Vernie twisted my right arm behind my back and held me in that position while I struggled to gain my freedom and pleaded with him to release me. I finally escaped his grasp once his spindly little arms could no longer hold me. Club membership did have its rewards!

14

The Trash Run

Nearly every Friday during the summer months, Archie and Vernie would execute a trash run. We didn't have a trash service, and I don't think one was even available in our neck of the woods in the 1960s. Two of my older brothers oversaw waste removal. On Fridays, Archie and Vernie loaded up the back of my mom's 1958 Pontiac station wagon with trash and drove about a quarter of a mile to our self-proclaimed landfill that Dad had chosen. Mom's wagon had seen some living, and I have a plethora of good and bad memories involving that old car.

Once in a while during the summer months, our mom loaded us kids in her station wagon, and we would head to the hamburger joint at the edge of town. Going to the hamburger and malt shop was a welcome treat and greatly appreciated by everyone. That was our version of eating at a fancy restaurant, and it was the highlight of my week. At some point during our little excursion, someone would yell, "I claim all remains." That one phrase rewarded the first person to shout it out with receiving all the food or drink that the younger siblings couldn't finish. I was not sure how or when that started, but Mom always backed the one who requested the leftovers. It kept down some of the bickering that was characteristic of our family.

I never won, considering I could barely finish my cheeseburger with everything, fries, and delicious chocolate malt.

On our way home from town one evening after dark, my mom was driving when a whitetail deer bolted out in front of the old station wagon. She nailed that deer and damaged the front end of the car to such an extent that we had no working headlights. Mom freaked out and cried because she didn't know how we would get home with no headlights. Archie jumped in to help and help he did. He rewired one of the headlights, so we had enough light to creep on home. His knowledge of science was not always used for nefarious purposes.

Other times during the summer, Mom loaded everyone in the station wagon, and we would head to the drive-in for a movie. My dad seldom went with us, and without him attending, it was like not having a police department. He always made us toe the mark and walk the line whenever we were with him. Before heading out for the drive-in, Mom would stock us up on popcorn, soda pops and whatever other movie snacks were available at home. We couldn't afford to buy snacks for the whole family at the drive-in-theatre because it would have cost a fortune with so many of us. The smell of the cheeseburgers and fries cooking at the concession stand made me long for the money to purchase some of that delicious food, but poor people have poor ways, and we were stuck with what had been brought from home. We appreciated it just the same and would not have missed it for the world. Those were some especially good times in that old car.

Back to the weekly trash run; Archie and Vernie had loaded a week's worth of trash into the back of that old Pontiac station wagon. Garbage from eight people was never a small amount. Archie was only fourteen at the time and had no driver's license. He and Vernie headed down the gravel road that passed by the front of our house. I wasn't allowed to go because I was too young, or so they said. Vernie was allowed to go because he was big enough to unload the trash from the car while Archie waited in the driver's seat for him to complete his task. He backed up to the small ravine and told Vernie to get out and get his job done. When the small ravine got a big enough pile of trash in it, my dad would bring a quart jar full of gasoline from the shed and douse that heap of trash. I witnessed a few fire balls over the years when that quart of gasoline was poured out and lit. The accompanying blast was like a small bomb exploding. I knew to keep my distance after seeing the explosion it created. That was how our landfill worked in the 1960s.

On the way back from that ill-fated trash run, Archie was hot-rodding Mom's car and fishtailing down the gravel road. Vernie, of course, screamed like a little girl, and Archie would drive crazy just to hear him beg and scream for him to stop. Stop he did! Archie lost control of the car and ran head-on into a large oak tree at the edge of the gravel road. The impact of a 4000-pound car did not budge that tree the least bit. I was at our house when the crash occurred and heard the thunderous collision. A few moments later, Vernie came scream-ing and running down the gravel road toward the house in a sheer panic. He cried out that Archie had crashed the car into a tree and his nose was gone. Archie had totaled my mom's station wagon and was slowly making his way back on foot.

As soon as Vernie told us the news, we all headed out to find Archie, who was now nearing the house. Even from a distance, the blood on Archie's face and white T-shirt was evident. As he drew closer, I could see how badly his nose was broken. His nose was pushed up and looked flat, like a pig's snout, with blood flowing everywhere. He told Mom that a dog ran out in front of the car, and he swerved to miss it. *Yeah right!* Mom was flipping out because that car was our only means of transportation when Dad was at work, and Archie needed to see a doctor immediately. I was horrified at the sight of his mangled face, but I could not look away. Mom began frantically calling neighbors to see if they could rush Archie to the hospital. The first one she called agreed and came right over.

Upon arriving at the hospital, the doctor set Archie's nose, but it was never again that petite nose he had been born with. His new nose made him look like a prize fighter. The car wreck gave him a much wider nose and an ever-present reminder to drive safely. That was the last time the 1958 Pontiac station wagon was driven. It was hauled to a farmer's field in the area, and there it sits to this very day. That old car had witnessed the best and worst times and went out with a bang that the whole family will forever remember.

15

Christmas by Mom

Christmas at our home was a production put on by my cherished mother. We had very little money, but Mom always made Christmas a treasured time for all of us. The first thing on the to-do list was locate the perfect Christmas tree in the woods next to our home, cut it down, and drag it back to the house. Our tree selection was simple, seeing we had cedar trees growing all through the woods surrounding us. There were no fir or pine or spruce trees, just cedar trees sprinkled in among all of the oak, hickory, maple, dogwood, pecan, and many others. Cedar trees produce a wonderful, soft aroma with balsamic undertones, cooling scents and always, when smelled, sends me back in my mind to memories of Mom and family at Christmastime. My dad was typically in charge of cutting down our tree, but not always. Mom was more than capable of handling such a task.

Every fall, Mom would walk the 200 yards to our pecan grove and climb each pecan tree. Then, while up in the treetops, she would shake the limbs like a wild woman to knock the nuts to the ground, and I and all my siblings would gather them into bags. She used the pecans for making Christmas candies and baked goods. She was Super Mom!

Like I said, cutting down our Christmas tree was ordinarily Dad's task—his only task—in preparation for Christmas. He supervised cutting the tree and hauling it back to the house and securing it in the tree stand. His only job now done, he kicked back in his chair and watched as the rest of us work the Christmas magic. All of us wanted to help with hanging the ornaments, but in the1960s, most of the ornaments were made of thin, fragile glass. Mom learned from past years that if we helped, ornaments would be sacrificed. She in turn would hang the delicate ornaments and lights, and we were allowed to help with the fake icicles and canned spray snow and any indestructible ornaments. Christmas stencils and aerosol cans of spray snow emboss the windows with pretty designs. Snowy images of Santa Claus, snowmen, snowflakes, reindeer, and whatever other wintery likeness we desired were portrayed on the windowpanes. With Christmas music playing in the background as we decorated, we thoroughly enjoyed decorating while listening to Bing Crosby, Nat King Cole, Andy Williams, Frank Sinatra, Perry Como, Brenda Lee, Ella Fitzgerald, and Burl Ives, just to name a few. I especially enjoyed "Have a Holly Jolly Christmas" by Burl Ives. I can still remember the smell of that fake snow, and how it always reminds me of enchanting times and the wonderful sights and joyful sounds of the Christmas season.

Mom took care of all of the Christmas shopping, and how she kept those gifts hidden from us until they were wrapped was a wonder to me. We would nose around everywhere for our presents. After they were wrapped and under the tree, we would still shake them to figure out the contents. If the shaking didn't work, we would do what we could to see beyond the wrapping paper. Mom knew from previous experience that extra scotch tape on all seams of the wrapping was the perfect solution. If we tried to loosen the tape and tear the paper, we would get busted. I figured out a couple of my gifts on occasion, but that was not the norm. She was talented at outsmarting us and would place a small present in a much larger box with newspaper for filler, or she would place some canned vegetables in the box for added weight which always fooled us. She was all about doing her best to keep our surprise gifts a secret until Christmas morning finally arrived.

With all the decorating, shopping, and wrapping, Mom still found time to prepare loads of homemade sweet treats for Christmas. She made divinity, a variety of fudge, chocolate-covered peanut butter balls, taffy, sugar cookies, and cakes and pies galore. Everything was homemade and chock-full of tender loving care. It got to the point where she had to hide the candy items, or they would be devoured in one day by her ravenous children. One Christmas season she was especially sneaky and hid all the homemade candy in our washing machine. We could tell that candy had been produced while we were at school because the entire house smelled delicious when we arrived home, and we craved some. Mom laughed at us and said confidently that we would never find it.

That was an awesome challenge, so each of us kids fanned out around the house in search of the delicious treasure. We couldn't find those delicacies on the first day, so the next day I decided to look everywhere that it shouldn't be. I had not explored long as I peered inside of the washing machine. Eureka! Heaps of candy for me. I had big plans that did not include any of my siblings. I was going to consume every tasty morsel before Christmas. Cameron found me hiding behind our house eating a piece of Mom's homemade fudge. She promptly threatened me with my life if I didn't tell her where the candy stash was. In no time at all, she was out back eating a piece of homemade divinity while I finished up my fudge. Before Cameron could finish her sweet treat, Vernie showed up.

Vernie threatened Cameron to give up the location of the booty. She did, and that was it for the secret candy stash. Mom caught Vernie with a piece of fudge as he was sneaking out the front door and moved the treasure trove to a new location. We never found it again before Christmas day rolled around. That stolen candy somehow tasted sweeter than normal.

Our custom was to open our stockings on Christmas Eve. Mom was the one who filled up Christmas stockings for each family member. These contained store-bought candy and some small, inexpensive toys. We enjoyed opening stockings in anticipation of the big haul on Christmas morning. My favorite stocking stuffer as a kid was when I received a whoopee cushion. I had loads of fun with that toy until I made the mistake of sneaking it into my dad's chair just before he sat down. When he plopped down, it blew the side out of my whoopee cushion, and it never worked again. There should have been a warning label against placing it under adults. Dad felt so bad about that blow out that he later bought me some Silly Putty to ease my pain. I enjoyed my putty until it became so loaded with hair and other debris that I had to trash it. I still enjoy a good practical joke!

Dad worked for a construction company as an estimator, and each Christmas, several of his clients would send gifts to his office. Some of those tasty treats were brought home for us to devour. We loathed the fruit cakes, and he always tried to convince us that they were delicious. Dad was the only one eating any fruit cake. The taste of fruit cake is burned in my memory like the taste of canned horse meat. Not a fan of either one. Our favorite goody from Dad's office was a five-pound box of Russell Stover chocolates that a client would have delivered. Dad would bring the entire box of chocolates home for us to eat. When that box of chocolates was opened, it was like Shark Week at my house. The feeding frenzy had begun. Everyone knew their favorites and scrambled to get some. My favorites were the dark chocolates with nuts and/or caramel. The Roman Nougat was another excellent choice. Dad had to intervene and bring some sense of decorum to this yearly event. After a few days of kids sneaking into the lower layer of chocolates before the top layer was all eaten, there would be nothing left but those nasty creams and other less desirable candies. They were all sooner or later consumed, but that detestable fruit cake was never touched except for what Dad ate.

Christmas morning never arrived soon enough for me. Five o'clock was never too early to rise and shine on Christmas morn. If one sibling woke up, then everyone was awakened. Like it or not, we were opening gifts. My parents would reluctantly get out of bed and accompany us to the tree. There were always heaps upon heaps of gifts under and around the tree. We would frantically check the name tags on gifts and toss them to the rightful owner. In a matter of minutes, it was all over with but the cleanup. Disappointment would come over me when I realized I had opened my last gift. I was hopeful that when the newness wore off my toys, that my siblings would tire of their presents, and we could share. No one wanted to share their brand-new stuff right away. We would invariably get bored with all the new toys and start a wish list for the next Christmas. I miss thumbing through those huge Christmas catalogs that Sears, JCPenney, Montgomery Ward, and so many others would mail out each year. I reveled in thumbing through those catalogs and circling everything that I wanted for Christmas and always signed *Billy* by each item. I did not want one of my siblings to receive any of my awesome gift choices by mistake. Today technology has changed so many of my favorite traditions, and I am glad to see that some retailers have brought back the Christmas catalog.

Christmas dinner was the meal of the year. For real! Dinner was most often at one o'clock in the afternoon. My mom spent hours upon hours preparing a plethora of food items while Dad sat in his chair watching TV and waiting. Our dinner menu was made up of turkey and dressing, mashed potatoes and gravy, sweet potato casserole, homemade noodles, pear salad, ambrosia salad, green beans, corn, homemade dinner rolls, and a host of pies and desserts. Far too often, my eyes were bigger than my stomach, and I loaded way too much food on my plate. Most of the time, Dad intervened and urged me to put food back, knowing I couldn't eat it all. Once everyone had filled their plates and started to eat, it became unusually quiet. Just give it a few minutes and someone was sure to spill their drink. Mom would rush to clean it up while Dad ate and barked out commands.

When all my siblings became adults, Mom continued this tradition until she was no longer able to cook for everyone. She always wanted to prepare everything so that no one had to bring any side dishes. During our adult years, guess who we waited on for Christmas dinner more often than not? Vernie! He was always late. We called him the night hawk because he was always out driving around and drinking beer all hours of the night. He would then sleep all day long if he could. This made him chronically late, and Mom always delayed dinner for him. Several times, Vernie wouldn't call or even show up while we continued to wait for his arrival. The entire family was always upset with him over that.

I sure do miss spending Christmas with my parents. Mom and Dad both died the same year at the age of eighty-four. They died just three months apart after having been married sixty-four years. Christmas at my house was always filled with happy memories, thanks to Mom's loving desire to make it special for each one of us!

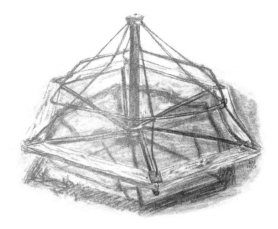

16

Grade School

Our school, as I mentioned, was small with only twelve students in my class. The building was a three-story wooden and brick structure that was infested with termites. The old wooden stairs in the building made a dreadful creaking noise each time we climbed them. (The building was eventually condemned and torn down because of extensive termite damage.) Even with a population of only about 600 in my hometown, there was always something outlandish happening at school on any given day.

There was a day in third grade when my friend, Orson, didn't feel well. He told Mrs. Smith that his stomach was upset, and he needed to go home. The oldest excuse in the book to get out of school and Mrs. Smith, in her usual style, told Orson he would be fine and to sit up and pay attention. As we lined up to go outside for recess, Orson informed the teacher a third time that his stomach was upset. Mrs. Smith told him he would feel better after recess. She was sadly mistaken. As we were about to head outside for recess, Orson bent over and showered a fountain of food all over the hallway floor in front of the entire class.

Jane caught a whiff of the vomit and started hurling! I was smart enough to get as far away from that smell as possible. Two others were not so fortunate as recycled lunch was being sprayed on the corridor floor. Half the class was gagging as if they were going to puke too. Mrs. Smith had made the wrong call again, like when she wouldn't allow me to use the restroom. There were no less than four students who caught that smell and spewed all over the floor. During the upheaval, Mrs. Smith was hollering for us to get outside to recess. Everyone felt the need to look and were each thoroughly repulsed. Tommy, our poor janitor, sprinkled some kind of dry mixture on those regurgitated puddles which smelled nearly as bad as what he was struggling to scoop up. He was still in the process of cleaning the floors when we came in from recess, and each of us held our breath as we passed by those stinky piles of throw up. It was back to business as usual once we had cleared the hurdles.

On another occasion, a girl in my class named Teri volunteered to push the merry-go-round during recess. She was stronger and tougher than the boys in my class. The old merry-go-round was pushed from a position in the middle, and if you tripped and fell while pushing, you better keep your head down. The steel bar construction held things together but would beat you senseless if you raised up while under the merry-go-round. Teri positioned herself in the middle and, like a thoroughbred stallion, was raring to go. Everyone piled on the wooden plank seats surrounding the exterior and held on for dear life to the steel bar in front of the seat. We were all excited, knowing it would be a thrill ride! Teri started out somewhat slow because of the extreme weight of so many kids that had crowded onto the ride. Soon the speed increased to a rapid rate.

Students screamed for her to slow down. I had seen Teri in action before, so I locked my arms around the steel bar and held on for dear life. She proceeded to go faster and faster until the world around us was simply a blur. She reached maximum speed and, instead of jumping up and riding, she continued pushing and running. Any normal person would have pushed a while and then jumped up and rode as the merry-go-round slowed down. But oh no, not Teri! That meant we were not slowing down, and anyone not locked on, as I was, would soon lose their grip and fall off. She kept running, and we were going so fast that the centrifugal force was spitting kids off left and right. Classmates were launched ten feet from the merry-go-round and skidding across the tiny white gravel which produced an excess of weeping and wailing from the casualties. Others begged her to slow down so they could get off. Teri was so proud of herself and her natural abilities, yet several of the other students were not so pleased. She was also very gifted at kickball and other sports and was always one of the first individuals chosen for teams.

Later that day, our class was on the playground for recess with some of the upper grades. Students were playing kickball, while others were swinging or climbing on the jungle gym. A girl from my older sister's class was swinging and trying to see how far she could jump as she leaped from the swing. On her third attempt for the farthest jump, her dress became entangled with the chain from the swing as she leaped for victory. It ripped her dress from her body and left her standing there in her underwear. I was shocked! Once the initial shock wore off, I hollered for everyone to look at Bonnie. They did, and we all had a good laugh at her expense.

17

Trick or Treat

Halloween was in third place at our house as far as celebrations went, only after birthdays and Christmas. We loved Halloween! Unlimited candy was always a welcome addition to our home.

My earliest recollection of trick or treating was when I was four years old. Mom supervised us as we dressed up in our costumes and headed out the front door to get free candy. *Free candy: can you believe it?* Every year at that time, people gave out free candy. *I love this country!* Mom drove us a mile or so to the nearest neighbor's house, and all six of us enthusiastically ran to the front door. On cue, we yelled, "trick-or-treat!" when the front door opened. Our neighbor, Mrs. Bradshaw, knew it was my family because there were so many of us. She called us her brown-eyed pea pickers. She was referring to our brown eyes, but I was never a pea picker, at least not yet. All of us kids had brown eyes, like my mom. Dad was the only one with blue eyes. Maybe that was why he never took us trick or treating. He was always odd man out with those blue eyes.

In the early years, my mom made our Halloween costumes, and she was pretty good at it. In fact, she was so good at it that those costumes lasted for years, and we tired of wearing hand-me-down costumes. She stitched together an organ grinder monkey costume, worn by two or three older siblings before I inherited it. I was the last one to wear that costume because it was on its last leg when I received it. The costume had a stupid-looking little round hat with a chin strap like an organ grinder monkey wore. The accompanying brown costume had a long tail, still attached by only a thread. I was as humiliated wearing it as my older siblings had been, but if that was what I had to do to get tons of free candy, I was good with it. We begged Mom for store-bought costumes and masks like the other kids were wearing, but money was tight back then, so we settled for what was available. I suffered the same fate when it came to hand-me-down clothes. I was sick and tired of wearing my older brother's used clothes. I was the youngest boy, and the clothes of my brothers were well worn by the time I grew into them—just like the Halloween costumes I inherited.

Filling one's bag with treats was the main goal of this treasure hunt. Most homes would not allow you to reach into the candy bowl but would place into your bag what they considered to be an adequate amount. There were a few places we visited where they said, "Reach in and grab all that you want." We made a mental note of those houses and hit them up first every year. A wide array of candy was luscious, but there were also many less desirable goodies. Snickers, Payday, 3 Musketeers, Butterfinger, Tootsie Rolls, Sugar Daddy, Jolly Ranchers—all things store-bought were what we desired. Less sought-after treats like popcorn balls, cookies, Chex mix, and those big orange circus peanuts were the last things to be consumed. As well as black licorice. Mostly good stuff ended up in our bags, but not always.

When we arrived back home, everyone would go through their candy sack to identify the items they desired to trade out for something more to their liking. Vernie liked that nasty black licorice, and I traded my black licorice for just about anything, including a popcorn ball. Once all the swapping was over, then it was time for everyone to hide their stash. You had to hide your Halloween candy. If Vernie or Helga found your stash, they would steal all or part of it, depending on how hungry they felt at the time.

Just as Mom was so great at planning Christmas, she also went above and beyond to make Halloween a fun and exciting time for each of us. She did what she could to keep the older kids out of our candy but with limited success.

18

Dear Ole Dad

My dad was one of a kind! I considered him to be a mixture of John Wayne and Archie Bunker. People either loved my dad or hated him. There was no straddling the fence when it came to him. For better or worse, I dearly loved my dad, but he was opinionated, and his opinion, like it or not, was the correct one. Whenever one of us boys misbehaved, Dad would tell us he was going to set up a boot shop in our butt or the often-used phrase, "Son, you are going to be digging my boot out of your butt!" He was always threatening to *rackie cack* one of us. I was never sure what that phrase meant but was positive that I wanted no part of being "rackie cacked!" He also enjoyed telling us that he would put a knot on our head big enough to wear a hat on. If you weren't attractive then, according to Dad, you must have been beaten with the ugly stick. He was famous for his one liner.

There were days when one of us kids would tear something up or leave one of Dad's tools out in the rain after working on a bicycle, and when he discovered the damage and questioned us, no one would admit guilt. Whoever committed the crime was not confessing.

Dad's solution to punishing the perpetrator was to line us up and spank every one of us. If no one fessed up, then we all got it. I still think the perp was either Vernie or Helga. They prided themselves on getting the rest of us in trouble. Either one would lie to get out of a paddling. "Sweetie Pie," Monica—the youngest and likely the most innocent—escaped Dad's lineup. Then he would pull that thin leather belt out of his belt loops, and the sound it made would put a knot in my throat and stomach as I anticipated those fiery swats. He held that belt doubled over in his right hand as he took each one of us by the left hand. It was quite a dance, the running in circles, scream-ing and crying while the other siblings waited in terror and antici-pated their time on the dance floor. I never could outrun that belt but finally got smart enough to avoid it by not doing stupid stuff, at least I tried to cut back on my stupidity.

When Dad was home for dinner, fooling around at the dinner table was not tolerated. The evening Vernie shoved my face into a plate full of hot mashed potatoes and gravy, Dad—the crime deterrent—was not home. On many a night, Dad would say, "Let's get our rain-coats on and head to the dinner table." He knew someone was bound to spill their drink and we did our best not to disappoint him.

My poor mom was hard pressed to ever be allowed to sit down and enjoy a meal with the family. She was always up and moving around, getting whatever anyone requested. Dad was worse than us kids when it came to being needy. If the salt or pepper was not on the table, Dad would say, "Maddie, where's my salt? You know I need salt with my meal." Or another was, "Maddie, where is my tea? You know I need a drink with my meal." Mom would get up and get him whatever he had a hankering for. She was a really great person! I always thought Dad could get that stuff himself but never vocalized those thoughts.

On many a Sunday, Mom fried a whole chicken for dinner, and she ended up eating the back, which had little or no meat on it and was by far the worst piece of fried chicken. She said she liked the back, but I knew she was leaving the best pieces for everyone else. That's the kind of mother she was, giving and loving by nature. Dad, on the other hand, was cut from a different cloth. He would go to the store and buy one T-bone steak. We couldn't afford to purchase T-bones for everyone, so Dad would buy one, *just for himself.* After he charred the steak on his charcoal grill, he would sit down at the table and eat alone while I watched like a starving dog, waiting for whatever remained of the one-man barbecue. The bone was always available afterward, and I would gnaw on that bone until the final remnants of meat were removed. I still like a good T-bone steak and think of Dad every single time I consume one.

One evening when there were eight of us around the dinner table, Monica piped up and said she had a joke to tell. She was six years old and still had much to learn about life. My dad was all ears while his Sweetie Pie told her joke. She said, "There was a girl who was so skinny that she had to rat her hair to keep her pants up." The look on Dad's face was priceless as my older siblings cautiously laughed. Dad was shocked and asked Monica if she knew what that meant and where she had heard the joke? She said no and could tell from the expression on Dad's face that it was not a clean joke, then she hung her head in shame. Dad proceeded to explain to her that if she didn't know what a joke meant, then she better not retell it. Later that evening, I asked Archie what it meant. He for sure knew, and then I realized why Monica should not be retelling that joke. We never did find out where she heard it. I still think it was one of Archie's puns because he enjoyed telling me that Vernie was born a twin. He said that the baby boy died but the turd lived. I didn't get that joke for years but still thought it was funny because Vernie acted like a turd.

Going to church was an event for which Dad did little to help prepare. On Sunday mornings after Mom finally got me and my siblings cleaned up and dressed, she would get herself ready. She tried to keep all of us inside the house while she dressed so we wouldn't get our church clothes filthy while playing outside. Dad dressed himself and was always ready early so he could sit in the car and smoke cigarettes while periodically honking the car horn in an attempt to speed up Mom. She got so angry at him for that. He never helped get us clothed, and I don't remember him ever changing a diaper on any of us. It all fell on Mom's shoulders. Filing out of the house behind Mom, we then loaded up into our Pontiac station wagon. Our crew could fill up a car faster than a Chinese fire drill!". Mom complained that she was going to smell like cigarette smoke, and she didn't know why she even bothered with perfume because she smelled like an ashtray. Off to church we went!

Don't even think about having fun while Dad is in the car. If he had to pull the car over, then someone was going to get it. You also didn't want to kiss the back of his hand when it came flying at you from the front seat. Kids were to be seen and not heard, according to him. When we arrived at our small Baptist church, we were supposed to be on our best behavior. *Good luck with that!*

Everyone knows that if you are where laughing is frowned upon, then everything makes you giddy. Something takes over, and you cannot control the silliness. Archie was always trying to get us to laugh during church. He made the goofiest faces at us while Dad wasn't looking. He was also very good at wiggling his ears. That was a real crowd pleaser. If Dad caught you acting up in church or laughing, he would say, "You think that's funny? I'll show you something funny." A spanking was waiting for you at home and that was no laughing matter.

Dad was a no-nonsense kind of guy. He and his three brothers fought in WWII. His oldest brother was only nineteen when he was killed on the USS Arizona at Pearl Harbor when the Japanese attacked. My uncle's body is still entombed in the USS Arizona, and his name is on the memorial. I am sure that losing his oldest brother at such a young age and losing a younger brother to suicide ten days before I was born had a tremendous impact on my dad's life. He was always looking out for our best interest, but many times I just couldn't see past the smoke of his rhetoric.

19

Super Mom

I could never give too many kudos to Mom! Long before I ever came along, things were difficult for her. Her father died of a heart attack at the age of thirty-eight. That left my mom, who was only ten years old at the time, and her three younger brothers with no one to support the family. Her mother found it impossible to provide for four young children during the Great Depression. Times being as difficult as they were, my grandmother took my mom and her three younger brothers to the county courthouse, informed the powers that be that she did not want these children anymore, and left them there all alone to be placed into foster care! My mom was a mere twelve years old when this horrid event took place. I can't even begin to imagine how she must have felt. Losing her beloved father just a few years earlier, then being discarded like a bag of trash. She never forgave her mother for abandoning them!

I remember an older lady coming to our house in the woods when I was around four years old. There was a knock on our front door, which was a rarity. We seldom had visitors, so it was highly unusual for someone to be knocking at our door in the middle of the day. I hid behind Mom's skirt, holding on for dear life as she answered the front door. I could tell that she knew this unfamiliar woman because she immediately asked her what she was doing there and why she had come by? Mom was clearly shaken by this encounter. The short conversation ended with her telling this mysterious woman that she never wanted to see her again. The lady departed with those words, and I never saw her again, nor did my mom. I found out later that the lady was my grandmother.

As I grew older, Mom shared many things about her childhood. She often spoke of her father with glowing memories of what a great dad he was to her and her brothers and how she dearly loved him. It made me fight back tears as she recalled and shared some of the tumultuous circumstances that she was forced into. None of it was because of anything she had done. She had been at the mercy of her unfortunate circumstances and often spoke of how she tried to keep herself and her three younger brothers in the same foster home. They were eventually separated and placed into different homes, and she cried as she shared how heartbroken she was because she felt she had failed her family.

A few months before Mom and her brothers were officially abandoned at the courthouse, they were left by themselves in an old farmhouse way out in the country in northern Arkansas with nothing to eat but canned green beans and canned peaches. She was only twelve years old when this happened, and they were stranded there all alone, for two weeks! She did what she could to keep herself and her brothers from starving to death by heating up the canned green beans and eating canned peaches at every meal. Her mother had already put so many burdens on her, which involved taking care of her younger brothers, that she was somewhat prepared for these two weeks of abandonment. Her mother did eventually come back for them, but it was short lived. She discarded them at the county courthouse several weeks later for other people to raise them.

Mom also shared stories from her high school days. There was a girl by the name of Mary Jo who was always teasing and making fun of her. Mom was very naive about the world and just had a sweet innocence about her that others loved to exploit. I imagine the other girls were jealous because my mom was so pretty and popular but also very shy and humble. She was so popular that the students voted her queen at her high school prom! Mary Jo approached my mom in the school hallway first thing one morning and asked her if she wet her hair before coming to school. Mom said no, and Mary Jo and the other girls with her started laughing and said, "What did you do, pee through a straw?" Mom could see that she had been duped again and did her best to avoid those girls from that day forward.

Most everyone enjoyed spending time with my mom. Unlike my dad, she was not an acquired taste. She was beautiful on the outside and the inside, fun loving and was all for a good laugh. Dad, on the other hand, was so serious and much more reserved with his feelings. When my dad was in Burma during WWII, he had a picture of my mom in a flowery one-piece swimsuit that he proudly displayed for all to see. When the Burmese men would admire Mom's picture they would say, "Ding qua qua." Dad's translation was that they approved of her. Some of the other men would display pictures of wives and/ or girlfriends, and the Burmese men would say, "Boo how," which according to Dad translated, "Not good." Dad loved telling that story about his beautiful wife. The funniest jokes he ever heard were the ones that he told. At times he scolded my mom for being so giddy, but her youngsters loved her for it. She was the glue that held the family together. Mom did not want her children to go through the suffering she had endured because of a bad parent. She truly was the best! As I think back on all the dirty laundry washed for ten of us, all the meal preparation, and the cleanup with no dishwasher, all the canning she did in the fall, and a thousand other things that she did for me and nine other people, she was Wonder Woman!

A trip to the grocery store with Mom was always an adventure. For one thing, she wasn't the best driver in the world. Once, we were making our way across a narrow, concrete bridge when a tractor trailer rig entered the opposite end of the bridge. It was going to be tight when we met and passed by that big rig. All of us screamed as Mom scraped the passenger side of our Pontiac along the side of the concrete bridge trying to stay clear of that giant truck. We all survived except for the paint on the passenger side of the car. Mom was in serious trouble when Dad arrived home that day; he was not the least bit happy about the damage to the car.

Many a time when she was driving, us kids hid in the floorboard of the car or just covered our eyes so as not to see what was about to possibly happen. She argued that she was not that bad of a driver. We loved her dearly, but she couldn't drive without scaring us to death. She was one of those motorists who would turn around and talk to everyone in the backseat, and in turn, we would scream for her to turn back around and watch the road. She never saw a problem with that behavior, and somehow, we survived even without seat belts or car seats. Seat belts were optional for most of my childhood, and lying in the back window of the moving car was always a delight unless one of my siblings beat me to it.

When we entered the grocery store, I'm sure the store employees dreaded our arrival. Mom took us younger kids to the store and left the older ones at home. Far too often we arrived at the store thirty minutes before closing time, and we had at least an hour's worth of shopping to do. The store employees did not appreciate it when my mom acted as if she had no concept of closing time when it rolled around; she continued shopping as if there was no rush to exit the store. We could fill two shopping carts with both the top and bottom baskets stuffed to the brim. She must have thought since we were spending a small fortune, it didn't matter if we kept the store employees past their scheduled quitting time.

My siblings and I were ninjas when it came to slipping snacks and boxes of cereal that contained a special prize into the cart without Mom noticing. The trick was to distract her at the register when your items were being rung up. If she saw an unfamiliar item, it was removed, set aside, and not purchased. I would hide several items in the cart, and typically enjoyed at least one of them upon arriving home. Siblings were always a concern during this covert operation. If Helga's items got nixed, and she saw my items going through, she would rat me out to Mom, and my items would not be purchased. I had to be super stealthy to get anything as a youth. We would never dream of attempting such a feat with Dad present. None of us had a desire to find out what it meant to get rackie cacked. Bag after endless bag of groceries would be hauled home every week.

It cost a living fortune to feed all of us. Mom clipped coupons from newspapers and magazines and filled up large bags with those coupons. Most of the time, whatever Mom was buying, she had a coupon for that product in one of the many sacks stored in our shed. She was always digging in those large bags of coupons, and it saved us tons of money. She also saved the proof of purchase seal on products, and if she needed twenty or more Tide washing detergent proof of purchase seals, there were usually more than enough since she washed a ton of laundry each month. She received ten uncirculated Morgan silver dollars from Tide using the proof of purchase seals from the detergent boxes. Decades later, I purchased them from her, and they are among my most prized possessions from her. She was always receiving promotional items from companies that appreciated her business. Mom was a businesswoman in her own right even though she was a stay-at-home mom.

Summertime lunches with all my clan home from school was a genuine challenge for mom. On most days during the summer, we dined on pickle loaf or bologna sandwiches with cottage cheese and canned pork and beans. A grilled cheese sandwich with a cup of Campbell's tomato soup was also a delicious lunch. Mom worked as quickly as possible to get lunch on the table, but it was never fast enough for us. There would be six of us seated around the dinner table, banging our fists on the table while chanting in unison, "We want to eat! We want to eat! We want to eat!" Archie, being the oldest in the house at the time, was the ringleader. At Archie's command, we put our spoon in one hand and fork in the other while banging our fists on the table in sync and chanting, "We want to eat!" Mom would say, "You kids are driving me crazy." As if that wasn't enough aggravation for her, we would argue over who got the tiny piece of pork fat that was in every can of pork and beans.

We also argued about who got to drink from the Reddy Red glass. There was only one red aluminum tumbler in our set of multi-colored drinking tumblers, and we all wanted the red one. We acted as if it were the Holy Grail. When lunch was finally placed on the table, the chants and commotion would cease except for one individual. Vernie, while eating, would growl under his breath. It was like eating next to a starving dog. He eventually outgrew that behavior, but even as a young child, I thought it was strange. I learned about supply and demand at a young age. Mom would have been a great referee or umpire because she quickly settled disputes each and every day.

Mom, even though she had a daunting number of chores to complete each day, found time to teach all of us how to pray. She would have us kneel next to our bed each night, and we would say, "Now I lay me down to sleep. I pray the Lord my soul to keep. If I should die before I wake, I pray to the Lord my soul to take. God bless Momma, Daddy, Ruby, Leroy, Archie, Vernie, Cameron, Billy, Helga, Monica, Fatty, Tippy, Smokey..." ... and any other cat, dog, bird or miscellaneous animal we had taken in that day. Then we ended with a hearty, "Amen." Mom was forever steering us in the right direction! For someone who had received so little love, she was rich in kindness and compassion and shared that with everyone she knew.

20

Green Acres

Enter the 1970s! My family moved from our 900-square-foot house, in which nine of us lived for five years, into an old farmhouse that was maybe 1200 square feet in size. This house was about two miles from town, which brought us somewhat closer to civilization and we no longer had to cross that swinging wooden deathtrap of a bridge. At that time, I was an avid bicycle rider, and would sneak into town on my bike to visit my friends from school. That was a plus, but this old farmhouse wasn't much better than what we had just moved from. All I could say was, it must have been cheap rent. Each of us referred to that place as "Green Acres," like the dilapidated old farmhouse in the TV show of the same name.

Dad performed some work on the house before we moved in, which was a minor improvement. Mom's younger brother always said, "The day your dad moved into a house was the best that house ever looked." He was poking fun at my dad who never did any maintenance once he moved into a house. It was a steady deterioration process that Dad never interrupted, even though he had spent his whole life in the construction industry and could fix nearly anything. If something around the house broke but did not affect him directly, then it was certainly not a priority. I am exactly the opposite of my dad in that regard. I witnessed on several occasions how those nonfunctioning items had a direct negative impact on my sweet mother, and Dad took forever to repair what would have made her day or week or even year less difficult. I run a much tighter ship at my house, and my wife thanks me all the time for taking care of her needs. Genuine love is a great motivator!

Moving my mom to that new location was not an easy task. Once she put down roots somewhere, it was difficult to get her to consider moving again. Knowing that she had been moved around from house to house while in foster care as a child made me sympathetic to her plight. Sometimes a move is necessary, and that one most certainly was.

That old two-story farmhouse was located right next to where the landlord, Mr. Woodson, raised his hogs. That's right, we moved to a hog farm! The hog pens were on the north side of the house, and encircling the rest of the house were field after field of corn. A large, red barn sat on the property that must have been thirsting for a coat of paint for at least twenty years.

There was also a one-story concrete block building next to the barn used for storing the fall harvest of shelled corn. Our landlord ground up the corn kernels and mixed it with bone meal and several other ingredients to produce hog feed used to fill the creep feeders. The hog house and creep feeders were also on the north side of our house. Pigs wallowed in large mud holes in the hog lot and were constantly, day and night, feeding while at the creep feeders. Those feeders were about eight-foot tall and round with an eight-foot diameter, encircled with metal lids all around the base. The pigs would lift the lid with their snout so they could get to the feed and eat. When a hog was done eating, it would simply back away from the feeder and the lid would drop down to the closed position with a loud "clang." That went on nonstop all day and all night. Every. Stinking. Night!

It took me months to be able to tune out that constant clanging of the feeder lids at night so I could get some sleep. Because the noise was constant day and night, it was worse than living next to railroad tracks.

The smell from the hog lot and hog house that was only a few hundred feet from our *mansion*, was atrocious! I loathed it when the wind came out of the north because it blew that stench directly at and into our home. If the weather was dry, the hogs kicked up the dust in the lot, and it drifted into the open windows of our residence. We had no central air conditioning, so the windows were always open when the weather was warm. After an abundance of rain, the hog lot reeked even worse, and that odor permeated everything.

When people came to visit for the first time and stepped from their car, they always asked, "What is that smell?" It goes without saying that folks were not overly eager for a second visit to Stinky Ville. I always got a charge out of each time my mom's younger brothers came. Her youngest brother smoked cigars and was quite a jokester. There is an old wives' tale that says, "If you see a hog carrying a stick in its mouth, it's going to rain." When I saw my uncle smoking a cigar, I told him it was going to rain because a hog was carrying a stick in its mouth. He didn't see the humor in it like I did.

We did have a little more space in this dwelling. A big bonus. My oldest brother was out of college and on his own, so that left six kids and two parents in this ragged old house. It also had a water well instead of a cistern, which was a major improvement. With every advantage there is usually an associated disadvantage. We had a water well, but the downside was the old, galvanized water pipes in the house. They should have been replaced years ago with copper lines. Those old pipes were decomposing so badly that little black specks from the interior of the pipes flowed out with the water from the faucets. Those little black specks left black marks on whatever they encountered. Black specks settled to the bottom of the bathtub and smeared on your butt cheeks—which defeated what you were trying to accomplish by bathing. My solution to the problem was the "Billy Weird Final Filter" named after me because I was the first to utilize that amazing invention at our new digs. I tied an old rag over the spout of the faucet in such a way that it filtered out the black specks. If this was not used, then you ended up with a bathtub full of water with black specks all over the bottom. Our water was like that for the entire twelve years we lived in that house. Who knows how many of those black specks my family drank each day while living at that location. Fortunately, none of us are suffering from any bizarre ailments due to consuming those contaminants.

We also had a fruit cellar like the one in the movie *The Wizard of Oz*. It was a stone and concrete underground structure that was barely covered with dirt. It looked like a dirt mound with a door. The underground interior was a mere six feet by eight feet and overcrowded when we were all in there during a thunderstorm. The cellar ordinarily had about twelve inches of standing water in it after a rain and was a haven for spiders, mold, and anything else that liked a dark and damp environment. Spending time in that cellar during a thunderstorm was never a good experience. With water seeping in and spiders everywhere, I felt more secure in the house during a storm. If Dad said, "Let's head to the cellar," then we all headed to the cellar even if it was three o'clock in the morning. Dad loved to sing this song to us about sliding down my cellar door and being jolly friends for evermore. He did have a fun side to him, but the pressure of raising and providing for eight kids put a considerable amount of stress on him, therefore his fun side was seldom seen. Dad was typically more on the serious side than jovial, and every one of us was delighted when his comical side made a rare appearance.

21

The Garden

When we lived in the little house next to the woods, my dad's garden wasn't very big. It must have been because the soil in that area was too rocky and hard. He was particular about his garden, and when my older brothers got into a green tomato fight while he was at work, he went ballistic on them for wasting his tomatoes. After we moved to the new location at the hog farm, Dad went hog wild when it came to garden size. Farms in the area were filled with crops such as corn, milo, soybeans, and wheat because the soil was tillable. Dad used our landlord's tractor to plow and prepare a new garden spot. His latest garden was ten times the size of the garden at our previous location. I grew to hate small scale farming! It was the responsibility of Mom and us kids to keep that gigantic agricultural project tilled and weeded. Helga whined so much that she would oftentimes be excused from the work. Vernie would purposely do such a poor job that Dad didn't want him helping either. I figured Dad didn't want to deal with all the whining. Even when Helga and Vernie did help, they weren't much help.

Planting time came in early May each year and was not something I anticipated with delight. On Saturday mornings, Dad would per-suade all of us to get out of bed around eight o'clock, even though we all wanted to sleep in. I hated that garden and to this day, I do not have a garden. We planted a wide variety of vegetables with Dad supervising and giving rise to a whole bunch of shouting. When an adult has one kid helping them, it equates to having one kid help. When two kids help, it's like having half a kid help. When you have three or more kids helping, it's like having no help at all because they are busy with anything and everything that has nothing to do with the work at hand. Dad was trying to get six of us steered in the right direction, and for Dad, it was like herding cats. We were all over the place and into everything once he turned his back on us and we were out of his line of sight.

We planted green beans, tomatoes, potatoes, okra, green peppers, eggplant, turnips, corn, cucumbers, lettuce, spinach, and whatever else Dad had a hankering to sow. The maintenance of all these plants was a daunting task! I spent at least twelve hours tilling the garden just getting it ready for the big planting day. That meant I was in the garden by myself, doing all this tilling for a minimum of a full Saturday and several evenings before the planting even started. He had me do the tilling instead of Vernie because he would purposely do a terrible job, so Dad eventually refused to utilize him. He thought it was funny that I had to do all the tilling and he was awarded a pass. Did I mention that I hated this garden? Like I said, on planting day there was plenty of hollering, all coming from Dad. He wanted those rows as straight as an arrow. He hammered a steel stake at each end of each row and tied a braided nylon string between the stakes as a guide for making the furrows as straight as possible in which to plant the seeds. He had been in the construction industry his entire life, and during WWII he built airstrips in Burma. He wanted things precise, and we were not allowed to deviate from his masterful gardening plans. Whoever was digging the furrows had better keep them straight as the string that was a foot above the ground for a guide.

On our first planting at the new house, all six of us kids were in the garden to help. Dad was preoccupied at the other end of the garden with Archie, Vernie, and Cameron while Helga, Monica, and I were at the opposite end of the garden. We were supposed to be planting green beans into the long straight furrow that Archie had dug, but I had other plans. One of our cats had given birth to a litter of kittens several weeks prior, and the kittens were in the garden next to where we were working. I carefully placed three of the kittens in the soft soil and buried them up to their necks so all that was visible were their little meowing heads. All the meowing was in protest of being buried. I told Monica that I was growing cattails, which were an actual type of plant that grew wild in the area. Monica found it humorous, and we had a good chuckle. Helga, on the other hand, was not so amused and darted to the other end of the garden to tattle to Dad that I had buried some kittens. She enjoyed creating problems for others. Dad was not at all amused by my antics, and I was severely scolded, but somehow did not get rackie cacked.

I spent the rest of that shift in the garden throwing dirt clods at Helga while her back was turned. Monica loved it! She was always my favorite. On many occasions, Monica and I would lie in the grass next to the garden and play dead, hoping the buzzards circling overhead would pay us a visit. The turkey vultures never came down to feed, but we were entertained just the same.

After Dad supervised the planting, he was done until harvest time. Mom and all the kids were counted upon to keep the garden in tip-top shape until the veggies were ripe and ready for harvest. That meant an abundance of tilling between the rows for me and plenty of weeds to pull by hand from the endless rows of plants. We grew so many vegetables that Dad ended up giving most of our produce away to his friends and colleagues from work. Mom canned all the produce that she could, and what we didn't eat was given away. Dad received kudos for the free veggies, which I might add were top-notch. Our vegetables were substantially larger than normal since we fertilized them with horse manure, and the tomatoes were much larger than anything you would find at the grocery store. I am still waiting for my kudos.

22

My Friend Pierre

Moving to Green Acres definitely had some sweet benefits. We lived much closer to town, and we were out of the woods, literally. There were also neighbors nearby with kids to hang out with—a nice change from my siblings. Life was progressing nicely for me at this new location.

When we moved to Green Acres, we brought my dad's two bird dogs and a few cats. My siblings and I wanted our own dog to play with because Dad's bird dogs were for hunting, and he trained them just for that. Dad had a cousin who raised dogs, and she lived nearby. We visited her kennels and picked out the cutest little jet-black minia-ture French poodle that ever walked this earth. Our new puppy was adorable and full of vim and vigor. By consensus our new family member was named Pierre because of his rich French heritage. As a puppy, Pierre was so playful and loving that he was all I needed to be happy. Just to see him each morning put a huge smile on my face, and for some reason, I spoke baby talk to my small friend. Once the novelty wore off having a new puppy in our midst and Pierre grew up, my siblings were less and less inclined to pay much attention to him, and he became my pet.

When full grown, he was a wee bit larger than a Pomeranian, but not much. My mom held a special place in her heart for Pierre too. She loved him, like I did. With my siblings' interest in Pierre waning, that gave the two of us more one on one time to become the best of friends. I loved that little black ball of fluffy fur! He was a farm dog and not a show dog, so he was rarely groomed and became this mass of tangled and matted black fur. If ever Pierre received a trim, it was me doing the barbering since I had some previous experience with giving Helga such a stylish trim with the scissors. Pierre was groomed each spring and summer and never in the fall because he was an outside dog and needed his winter coat for warmth. He was never quite sure how to react when the shears came out, but I calmed him down with comforting words. I was certain it was the tone of my voice and not my words that brought him comfort; after all, I was speaking English, and he was clearly a French poodle. All he understood was "blah, blah, blah," but it was a very calming "blah, blah, blah." I clipped his fur down to a half inch or so, and he appeared to be a much smaller dog with that mass of tangled hair removed. After his grooming, Pierre would run crazily in circles and then roll all over the grass in our yard. I was convinced that he felt as light as a feather with all of those clumps of matted fur removed from his small body.

Pierre and I went everywhere together on the farm. If I was outside, my faithful friend was by my side and ready for whatever adventure the day had in store for the two of us. When Pierre would hike his leg on something to mark his territory, I would follow suit and leave my mark too. I figured maybe, just maybe, it would keep my siblings from trespassing on my territory.

Chasing rabbits on the farm was something that my dog and I both totally enjoyed. We never had a shortage of cottontail rabbits while I was growing up. Even though Pierre was French, I taught him a few English words. Every day, I would ask Pierre if he wanted to "chase rabbits" and he would run in circles and bark wildly in anticipation of the hunt. *Rabbit* was definitely in his vocabulary. We never actually hunted rabbits, seeing that we never had a gun or any other weapon with us. It was all for sport and competition to see who could out-fox who, a boy accompanied by a dog or the lone rabbit. Together we would walk the fence rows on the farm and had done it so often that we knew all the little critters' favorite hideouts. Many times, I would see a bunny hiding in a brushy patch or in the tall grass next to the fence rows, poke a stick in to flush him out, and the chase was on. Pierre was in hot pursuit while yipping and barking like he had lost his mind. He was super manic when he got a look at that white cottontail hopping away just out of his grasp. I got a good belly laugh out of watching his exuberant antics.

We chased rabbits in winter, spring, summer, and fall. We even captured one little bunny, and it was my genius that trapped the little creature. We had chased that same bunny on many occasions; he outfoxed us and hid somewhere that we couldn't find him. That rabbit would double back on us, and we'd never see him again that day. I finally figured out that Mr. Bunny took the same escape route each day to outsmart us. He ran through the same exact spot in the wire mesh fence because that was the only spot big enough for him to squeeze through.

This quest was going to be different. A new day had dawned on the farm, and it was time to show this bunny that he had met his match. The day before we flushed out our bunny friend from his burrow, I went to that one spot in the wire mesh fence where he scurried through and eventually evaded us. I then squeezed the wires closer together, making it impossible for him to slip past. Let the games begin! We found our furry little friend in the same patch of brush as usual. I kicked at the brush a few times while Pierre went totally bonkers anticipating the chase. The rabbit burst from his hideout, and we were in hot pursuit. Our bunny was speedily hopping to his escape route in the fence, not knowing that it had been narrowed considerably. As he tried to squeeze through the fence, the smaller front portion of his body made it through, but his hips were too thick, and he was stuck and squealed like crazy.

Hearing the rabbit squeal sent Pierre into an even higher level of crazed excitement. I quickly released our bunny from the fence, unharmed but very skittish. I held him up so that Pierre could get an up close and personal look at the creature that had eluded us on so many outings. We were both so proud of ourselves because we had finally caught one. We released our little playmate after a few minutes and looked forward to seeing our buddy again and again in the near future. From that day on, whenever I would ask Pierre if he wanted to chase rabbits, he would go insane with enthusiasm, running in circles and barking like he had lost his mind. He provided a wealth of entertainment for me with his fantastical playfulness!

Wherever I went on the farm, Pierre was by my side. If I went to the creek behind our house, he was with me. If I walked down our long gravel driveway to the mailbox or traipsed through the cornfields, my little buddy was there by my side. Pierre was present and ready for whatever the day would bring forth.

We had a corn crib behind our house which was a single story, con-crete block structure used by our landlord to store the fall harvest of shelled corn. There were no corn cobs, just heaps upon heaps of shelled corn. Our landlord used the kernels of corn to grind up into hog feed. It was a blast to play in the corn crib which was three to four feet deep with corn kernels. Pierre thoroughly enjoyed this activity because there were numerous mice to chase in the corn crib and countless places for them to hide. Located inside the building were pieces of corrugated tin and scraps of plywood strewn about, and the mice loved to hide and or build their nests under these.

Pierre knew the routine by heart. I would grab the edge of a piece of corrugated metal roofing, and he would go bonkers while waiting for me to lift the tin and reveal the mice that would scurry out in all directions. Every now and again we uncovered so many rodents that Pierre didn't know who to chase. He got a charge out of pursuing those tiny rascals, and periodically he would let out a loud yelp because a mouse had bitten him on the nose. That did not discourage him in the least as we continued our mouse hunt. At times, the mice would have a nest of babies hidden under the discarded materials, and some were so young that they were hairless. Pierre would see the nest and gobble them down like Gummy Bears. We were an awesome team, and I was thankful for someone fun and warmhearted to hang out with. Life would have been rather boring without him.

Just to the south of our house and across a large cornfield, lived my school chum Orson. Before moving here, I had never had a friend that lived so close. Running parallel and right next to Orson's front yard was a blacktop state highway that I had to cross before entering his front yard. My mom and dad were concerned about any of their children being on that highway. We were forbidden to ride our bikes on that highway, so I walked to Orson's house.

I was forever cautious when it came to crossing that highway because people drove way too fast when topping the hill right next to Orson's home. He and I and most of the kids in our class attended school together from first grade through twelfth. I went to visit Orson quite often, and he came to my house on many a day. He had only one sibling, a sister, and not a slew of kids like my family. His parents had more disposable income than mine, therefore Orson owned all of the coolest toys. He had a small motorcycle that we often rode, and he possessed a real bow and arrows that we would shoot into hay bales. The first video game that I ever played was Pong at Orson's house and I was hooked on gaming from then on.

On one day, I walked across the freshly plowed field to Orson's house to see what he was occupied with. Pierre was never allowed to go with me because of the dangerous traffic on that state highway which passed adjacent to Orson's front yard. I was maybe halfway across the field when I noticed that Pierre was trying to be sneaky and follow me. I yelled at him to go home, and he turned around and ran back toward my house. I arrived at Orson's, and while we visited, on his front lawn, we both noticed Pierre had crossed the highway into his yard. Without first thinking, I hollered again at Pierre to go home, and he took off running toward the highway and home. I glanced down the highway, noticed a car coming in our direction, and hollered for Pierre to come back, but it was too late! I watched in disbelief as my dog ran in front of that car, and the front tire ran over his back. His back was immediately broken, and he used his front paws to pull his broken body off the highway and into the ditch, still attempting to get back home. Orson and I ran to his side, and he was still alive. Pierre looked up at me with his big brown eyes as if to say, "Please help me!" The car stopped, and the lady driving it felt absolutely horrible about running over my dog. I told her that it was my fault, and she could not have done anything differently. I bent over and picked up Pierre and cradled him in my arms to carry him home across the newly tilled field. That was the loneliest walk I had ever taken in my young life. About halfway across that field my best friend in the whole world died in my arms. His labored breathing stopped, and his small body went limp within my arms, and my spirit was consumed with sorrow. Heartbroken, I wept as I walked across that field while carrying the lifeless body of my dearest pal. I was only thirteen years old and had never experienced such grief or sense of loss in my entire life.

As I approached our home with Pierre's lifeless body enfolded in my arms, my sweet mother was seated on the back steps of our house and noticed me drawing near as I cried uncontrollably. She lovingly asked me what was wrong, and as best I could, I told her that Pierre had been hit by a car and was dead, and it was all my fault. Both of us were crying at that point as I laid his lifeless body on the ground next to my mom. I then took off running toward the creek behind our house because I wanted to grieve alone.

We buried Pierre later that day in our backyard with all my siblings and my mom in attendance. Dad was still at work, or he would have also attended. I was very distraught over losing my pet and Dad wanted to lend a hand. He purchased another black miniature French poodle that looked just the same, and we named him Pierre II. The new puppy was great, but he was not my rabbit chasing buddy. Pierre could never be replaced, and it was never the same again, at least for me.

23

Riding Bikes

A youth with a bicycle is a kid with freedom. I learned to ride a bike while living in the little house in the woods. That was in 1966, and the bike I learned to ride was an adult-sized, twenty-six-inch bicycle. If I was seated on the bike, my feet weren't even close to touching the ground. I was so small that, to ride the bike, I had to stand on the pedals because I couldn't reach them if I was seated.

Archie was kind enough to help me with that dilemma. He held me up on the bike and gave me a huge push, and off I went down the gravel road in front of our house. Not being able to touch the ground did not discourage me in the tiniest bit. I was bound and determined to ride that bike and was successful on my first attempt. When it came to stopping the bike, I would either fall over and get off or place both legs on the same side and jump off. None of that mattered to me because I now retained a newfound talent that would serve me well for years to come. As I grew taller and could easily touch the ground, I enjoyed riding my bike barefoot during the warm summer months. There were those instances when my foot would slip off the pedal and my toes would be chewed up by the gravel road. That was ever so painful, and yet I wasn't wise enough to wear shoes on my outings.

As I said before, moving from that little house in the woods to our current farm home placed me a mere two miles from town. We were forbidden by our parents to ride our bicycles on the blacktop state highway that ran past the farm. That rule was set in stone, for obvious reasons, and it didn't help matters that Pierre had been struck and killed by a car on that very road.

One warm summer day in July, I decided I would ride my bike into town to see the sights and hopefully bump into some of my school chums. There wasn't that much to see or take in, but I was intent on sneaking into town without my parents' knowledge. Helga noticed me sneaking off and wanted to go with me wherever I was headed. She knew being with me was always an adventure, but I didn't want any tagalongs. I told her I was headed downtown, and she was not invited. She threatened to tell Mom and Dad if I refused to indulge her request to accompany me. Helga had put me in a real pickle. Dad was at work, but if she squealed to Mom, then Mom would tell Dad and a spanking would be waiting for me that evening when Dad arrived home. This was a no-win situation for me. I should have just rescheduled my trip for another day, but the town was calling my name so loudly that I gave in to her request. Helga ended up riding with me into town, and I didn't care much for it.

On our way to the city, there was a large hill we had to pedal up, and it took all that our young legs could muster to get over that hump. That hill would be loads of fun on the way back. We could coast for a great distance while going down and save some energy on our drive back home. We made it into civilization just fine and said hello to some friends from school as we cruised down Main Street feeling ever so grown-up. I was always envious of my classmates who resided there, anytime they wanted, they could get together with all the other kids who lived in town. I was stuck with siblings with which to occupy my time.

Soon I realized we'd better not stay too late, or Mom would start to wonder where we had ventured off to. As we steered toward home, everything was going like clockwork until we topped the steep hill on the highway. We favored riding on that flat blacktop surface as opposed to the gravel roads in the area because we could truly sail while tooling along down that smooth veneer. The two of us were cruising right along as we climbed that big hill and started our descent. While both of us were headed down that hill, our bikes continued to pick up speed at an alarming rate! For some reason, Helga could not apply her brakes, and as I slowed down, she sped past me. I watched as she raced down that hill ahead of me, completely out of control. She was now at the mercy of the hill which seemed more like a mountain about to engulf her and her bicycle. That hill did not want her presence any more than I did.

She screamed, "Help me! Help me!" but there was nothing I could do other than yell, "Hit the brakes!" and watch and hope that she survived our expedition into town. She raced farther and farther ahead of me, and the front wheel of her bike began to shake erratically. When your wheels are not balanced properly and you reach a certain speed, then your bike will get what is termed *the speed shakes*. If you continue to increase your speed, then the bike wheels will wobble out of control, and you will crash. That was precisely what Helga became the victim of. Her bike convulsed so violently that she lost control, ran into the overgrown ditch at the edge of the highway, and flipped her bike and herself end over end through a quagmire of tangled brush.

And there she lay, crying hysterically and screaming at me for taking her into town. I encouraged her to get up and get back on her bike, but she was not budging until I told her that I thought I saw a snake in the weeds next to her. She scrambled out of the ditch while I pulled her bicycle back onto the highway. Somehow, she escaped any broken bones but had loads of cuts, scrapes, and bruises for her efforts. After much crying on her part—and even more persuading by me—she eventually got back on her bike. We had to ride home before Mom figured out that we were AWOL.

When we arrived back at the house, the first thing Helga did was tell Mom what had happened. *What the heck?* She clearly had her own version of the day's events as she explained to Mom that I invited her to go into town on our bikes, and it was all my idea. She convinced Mom that she never would have done such a thing on her own, and I encouraged her to come along. Mom swallowed that hook, line, and sinker. Helga had turned this all on me, and I knew beforehand there would be inescapable results if she was in attendance. Mom turned toward me and said those eight frightful words, "You just wait until your dad gets home." *Ugh!* Helga had burned me yet again.

Later that afternoon when Dad arrived home, I was the only one who received a spanking. I guess Dad figured all the cuts and bruises on Helga was punishment enough for her. He told me he couldn't believe how irresponsible I had been. That is why I thoroughly enjoy the memory of that bike shaking out of control and Helga tumbling end over end into that ditch. She'll think twice before she invites herself on another one of my adventures.

When I was thirteen, I received a brand-new bicycle for Christmas. Best Christmas present ever! I could hardly believe my good fortune. My shiny new bike was metallic green which just so happened to be my favorite color. It had a banana seat with a tall sissy bar behind it and high handlebars with long tassels flowing from the handgrips that waved in the breeze as I headed toward my next great escapade. It was awesome! I could ride like the wind and look way cool in the process. Freedom was calling my name. I souped up my new ride by attaching a playing card to the bike frame using a clothespin. As the wheel spokes rubbed against that card, it made a sound just like a motorcycle engine, or so I imagined. Could life get any better?

Feeling extremely feisty with this new bike under me, I challenged Cameron to a bike competition, and she accepted. The great bike race took place two weeks after Christmas, and we were to race to the end of our long, gravel driveway. The victor would have bragging rights from then on. Our gravel driveway ended at the gravel county road that passed by on the east side of our house. People drove far too fast on that road, and you had better look both ways before pulling out of our driveway. It didn't help matters that there were masses of large, overgrown trees and thick brush that filled the fence rows, blocking one's view of any oncoming traffic. Cameron thoroughly enjoyed humbling me when I made those outlandish challenges. She savored rubbing my nose in the reality that she had been victorious most every time. I was always filled with unreasonable hopes and dreams, and she perpetually took advantage of that fact. We raced off on our bikes from the house, both of us determined to prevail. I pedaled my guts out, struggling to defeat her. I was doing all that my thirteen-year-old legs could muster, and she was still pulling ahead of me. The eternal optimist was losing again. As we approached the county road at the end of the drive, for reasons unknown to me at the time, my sister abruptly stopped at the end of the drive, and I sped past her. I couldn't get my head around the fact that she just threw in the towel, and I would be triumphant.

So focused on defeating her, I failed to notice the car speeding down the county road in our direction. After a brief, and I do mean brief, feeling of exuberance, I slammed into the back passenger door of that speeding car as Cameron observed this surreal scene play out before her eyes. I recollect being ricocheted straight up into the air about nine feet and landing flat on my back on that hard, rough gravel road into a cloud of dust created by the passing car. My left leg was throbbing, and I thought it was broken. Cameron quickly ran to my side and asked, "Why didn't you stop?" I told her I was so focused on winning that I didn't see the car coming. Our neighbor lady was driving the car and her daughter, Naomi, was in the backseat. She finally got the car stopped and backed up to see if I was still alive. She was terrified to think that she might have killed someone and was so relieved to see me sitting up and very much alive. Naomi was looking straight at me from the back passenger window when I struck the side of their car and was launched into space. That moment in time is frozen in my memory, and I can still visualize that flabbergasted expression on her young face as I walloped the side of their vehicle.

After examining my leg, we concluded that it was not broken, just deeply bruised. The neighbor, along with her daughter and Cameron, helped me into the car and drove me the short distance back to our house. My mom was, of course, freaked out too but so thankful that I was all right. She didn't want anything to happen to her baby boy with those angelic eyes, as she so often described me. I survived that crash with some deep bruising on my left leg and a few scrapes, and I suppose that I won the race, but I didn't feel like a winner. If winning is this painful, then I would just as soon lose and feel good than win and be all busted up. In a strange sort of way, Cameron had bested me again. Mom was ever so thankful that I did not arrive at that county road a split second earlier, considering our neighbor lady would certainly have run directly over me, and my family would have been planning my funeral. Someone was watching out for me. At that time in my life, I had no clue who He was. The front fork and front wheel of my new bike were a mangled mess. I had destroyed the best Christmas present ever, just a few short weeks after Christmas. I had to go back to borrowing my older siblings' bicycles. Pride and arrogance will always bring you down.

24

Farm Life

Life on the farm kept this very active boy occupied, but I so envied the kids that lived in town. Seemed to me that city living was the way to go. You had access to stores and tons of other people, and paved streets were everywhere. I found myself in enough trouble living in the country, and living in the city would have provided far too many opportunities for my untamed episodes.

Farm living wasn't much different than residing way out in the timber. Our neighbors were few and far between at both locations. I still had plenty of wide-open spaces in which to meander aimlessly about.

One breezy summer day when I was eleven, I decided it would be a good idea to stroll around naked outside. We had no neighbors within shouting distance, and what siblings were at home at the time were inside the house preoccupied with watching *"Gilligan's Island"* on the TV. It must have been that unencumbered feeling of independence that I found attractive, so I stripped off my clothes and headed out the backdoor totally in the buff. I got a charge out of climbing trees, so I scrambled up a large maple tree that grew alongside our house and driveway. I enjoyed the sights and sounds from that lofty vantage point. While standing in the fork of the tree about ten feet high and naked as a jaybird, I spotted our landlord motoring up the driveway in his pickup truck. He was making his daily rounds, checking on his herd of swine in the hog lots next to our house. Our driveway passed directly by the tree that I was situated in, and as he drove by, he looked up and saw me butt naked and waving with a huge smile on my face. He smiled right back at me and just shook his head and laughed as he drove past. I was always full of surprises. You can't do that if you live in town! The running around naked, I mean, not the waving and smiling. Once he drove past, I headed into the house to get dressed. Anytime I saw him, I went out to see what he was up to that day.

Many times, he allowed me to help him with farm chores, and that kept me entertained and gave him some much-needed help for free. On this particular day, it was time to castrate the feeder pigs. Feeder pigs are young pigs that you fatten up to take to market. They are not used for breeding, and therefore don't require all of their body parts. I had never heard of this thing called *castrating* but was more than happy to help out. Mr. Woodson had me catch one of his small pigs and bring it to him. Then I helped him hold the poor thing while he took his knife and made a small slit in the pig's scrotum. Both testicles were popped out of the slit, and then Mr. Woodson cut the cords on each one and tossed the gonads aside.

Holy moly! What had I gotten myself into this time? Those little pigs squealed like crazy during the whole process. There were no pain meds of any kind used for the poor little pigs. He did, however, spray some purple stuff on the wound so no infection would set in. I would chase down another pig and deliver it to Mr. Woodson, and the shrill squeals would start all over again. One poor little piggy was cut too much and required a few stitches, all without any pain meds. I was so thankful I had the wherewithal to put clothes on before venturing out there that afternoon. I would like to keep all my body parts, thank you! The thought of that process always makes me cringe. Some people actually eat those removed body parts and call them mountain oysters. I have always declined any offers to eat those things.

On a different day on the farm, Mr. Woodson was working on the window trim in the boys' bedroom upstairs. As usual, I wanted to watch or help or anything that he would allow me to do. I was watching as he was about to nail a piece of wooden trim next to the window in my bedroom. Unfortunately for me, I was standing too close behind him as he drew the hammer back to start nailing. The claws of the hammer struck me just under my right eyebrow, and blood trickled into my eye and down that side of my face. He was extremely concerned that he had damaged my eyeball, but fortunately for me, it was just a flesh wound. A very free-flowing flesh wound! I sported a black eye for weeks afterward. This was yet another of those many idiotic circumstances that I had placed myself in. Somehow, I had escaped once again with only a few scars. I still have scars over my right eye.

When Mr. Woodson was working with the full-grown hogs, he made use of a livestock shocker to encourage them to go wherever he wanted. That was the 1970s version of our present-day tasers. That livestock shocker required ten D batteries from end to end that filled a two-foot-long tube. It was so powerful that when he pressed the shocker to the rear end of a 400-pound hog, they jumped forward to get away from that jolt of electricity as they let out a loud squeal. When Mr. Woodson was done working with the hogs, he would leave that livestock shocker in the red barn, which was close to our rental house. I was fascinated with that electric toy and took it from the barn after Mr. Woodson departed for the day. I wanted to see what all the fuss was about.

Monica, whom I really like, was in the wrong place at the wrong time on that day. I chased Monica all over the hog lot with a desire to test out my newfound toy. She was quick but not quite fast enough as she frantically scaled the wooden slat fence surrounding the hog lot in an attempt to escape her deranged older brother and his torture devise. She was intent on heading to the house and the safety of Mom, but about halfway up the fence, the lightning from the shocker caressed her rear end. She literally flew over that wooden fence, screaming uncontrollably as she ran for the house to tell Mom. I still feel bad about that one.

When I arrived at the house, Mom said, "You wait until your dad gets home." I fully deserved this spanking, and it was going to be a doozy. I had done this to the baby of the family, and she was Dad's "Sweetie Pie." I was toast! He would take extra special care to ensure that I paid for my crimes against his "Sweetie Pie." Later that day, after Dad arrived home, I told him that I was trying to further my knowledge of how electricity works, but Dad was not buying it as his belt caressed my young backside once again. Monica was upset with me for days after that, and I truly hated using her as my guinea pig. Helga just wasn't available for that experiment.

Imagine, if you can, the many tens of thousands of houseflies that called the hog farm home. There was hog manure scattered all over the hog lots and in the hog house. That was paradise for those winged creatures. My dad's solution to our insect problem was to sprinkle fly bait around that would poison and kill each one that consumed it. For some unknown reason, Dad thought it best to sprinkle the fly bait right next to the backdoor of our house. Nobody ever used the front door because my parents' bedroom was just inside the front door. Everyone used the backdoor! Dad scattered massive amounts of fly bait on the sidewalk next to the back steps of our house and then moistened it with water from the garden hose. This, of course, attracted even more flies to that busy location. When the backdoor was opened to enter, the flies would be swarming in the area near the door. It was awful! The flies that weren't swarming were either lying dead by the thousands on the concrete walk and steps or spinning in circles on the ground, because they were about to die from the poison. There were dead flies all over the place at our backdoor. That entrance was not the place to put that poison. We all tried to explain that to Dad, but right or wrong, he was always right. You did not argue with Dad! It was either, "yes, sir," or "no, sir."

Wild critters were everywhere on the farm. Watching *"The Beverly Hillbillies"* on TV gave me a good chuckle. Elly May had all kinds of pet critters, and that was precisely how I rolled. At one point, I had a pet rabbit, squirrel, raccoon, and even tried to raise a bobcat kitten that I found near the creek running past our house. Dad vetoed the bobcat kitten, and I had to return it to the wild. Most of my pets, for one reason or another, didn't stay around very long. I didn't keep any of them in a pen and it was commonplace for them to venture back out into the wild after they reached a certain age.

I had a pet blackbird for a short time. My blackbird just showed up one day and was as tame as a house pet. He must have jumped out of the nest a bit too early and was unable to fly. I called him Heckle after the cartoon character from the TV show *"Heckle and Jeckle."* It was a cartoon about two black magpies. My pet was not a magpie but close enough for me. Heckle started hanging out with me one day, and I could hardly believe that he wasn't afraid of me or my family. In return for Heckle's easygoing nature, I started feeding and watering him, and he was content to stay. We had several cats on the farm, so I had to protect my blackbird from their bird-eating nature.

Heckle thoroughly enjoyed riding on the handlebars of my bicycle as I tooled around on the farm. It always put a smile on my mom's face when she peered from the kitchen window above the sink and saw the two of us riding past on my bike. In the evenings, I would place him on the roof of our house for safety, and then I hurried out the next morning to see if he was still there. He would be on the roof, waiting for my arrival on each new day. Times were great with my newfound buddy, until one fateful morning when I scurried out to get Heckle off the roof. Black feathers were scattered all over the shingles. No Heckle. I was thoroughly disgusted! Another one of my pets had been taken from me. I was almost certain one of our cats had eaten him. I didn't know how one of our cats could have gotten onto the roof. Vernie probably put the cat up there because he was jealous of all the attention Heckle and I had received.

I enjoyed living in the great outdoors and have learned from experience that wide-open spaces trump city living!

25

Cat Girl

That brings me to the subject of cats. Monica loved cats more than any of us. As an adult, she has four large cats in her home. I refer to her as the Crazy Cat Lady. I even made up a test for her and anyone else to take who might question whether they suffer from this ailment. Here are the questions that I presented to her to see if she fits the profile:

Crazy Cat Lady Test

If you answer yes to three or more of these questions, you are a Crazy Cat Lady:

Do you have more pictures of your cats in your phone than pictures of family members?

Do you love to purchase shirts with cats on them?

Do you have three or more cats?

Do you make cat videos and dub your voice in?

Did you spend $500 purchasing a cat?

Do you sleep with your cats?

Do you snuggle with your cat or cats instead of your spouse?

Do you post pictures of your cats on Facebook, Instagram or anywhere else online?

Do you allow your cat to sit on your lap while you are using the toilet?

Do you ever wear a kitty necklace with matching earrings?

Do you dress up like a cat at Halloween or any other time during the year?

Does your cat ever appear on your Christmas cards?

Monica confessed that she is indeed a Crazy Cat Lady.

Let us get back to the plethora of cats that were on the farm. These were all outside cats because Dad wouldn't allow them past the back porch. They roamed freely everywhere but in our house. On cold days during the year, after parking the car, our cats would either climb on top of the front tires next to the warm engine or crawl into the engine compartment under the hood to get warm. Many times, on cold days when backing up the car, a cat would be run over because it had been laying on top of the front tire. Often, it wouldn't kill the cat but would break its back. The cat would then use its front legs to drag itself to a hiding place to die. If my dad witnessed this, he would instruct me to get a baseball bat and put that cat out of its misery. It sounds awful, but it was the most humane thing to do and ended their pain and suffering. There was no way to fix a broken back. Somehow, Vernie got out of this detail, and I would end up being the doctor of death.

At other times, one of us would drive the car into town for gasoline and to check the oil. When the hood of the car was raised to check the oil, a cat would jump out and scare us half to death. None of those cats ever made it back home because once that hood opened, that scared kitty would take off running to parts unknown, never to be seen again. Those were the lucky cats!

26

Like Father, Like Son

I've said it before and I'll say it again, Vernie, often, was given a pass when it came to being involved in Dad's schemes. I was always recruited to assist him on his projects. Vernie and Dad did not like each other, and that lasted clear up to and beyond my father's death. Vernie was a bit of a loner and was not into any sort of sports: hunting, fishing, baseball, basketball, or the like. So, there I was again, being recruited to lend a helping hand for one of my father's latest schemes. If nothing else, it gave me a good work ethic which Vernie lacked. Dad got me involved in some activities that I knew beforehand was going to be a recipe for disaster. I understood enough about Dad so as not to say or do anything that would contradict his plan.

There were many times I accompanied my father on a fishing trip with no other siblings present. This Saturday morning, we were out of bed at five o'clock and ready to make the three-hour drive to a lake in Arkansas. The drive was a long one, but Dad had his favorite country western music blasting on the eight-track player with the tunes of Charley Pride, Loretta Lynn, Mel Tillis, Marty Robbins, Tammy Wynette, and many others. I especially liked Charley Pride and his song "Kiss an Angel Good Morning."

We eventually arrived at the lake for some trout fishing. At that time, I was about thirteen or fourteen years old. It was a beautiful spring day, and the high temperature was supposed to be in the upper seventies. We drove down to the boat ramp but had to park and wait for other trucks with boat trailers to launch their watercraft. Dad and I walked down to the edge of the water while we waited, and I noticed a mother duck with five small ducklings following close behind her. I told Dad that I was going to catch one of those baby ducks. His casual reply was, "Son, I wouldn't mess with those baby ducks if I were you." I told him that it would be just fine and gave chase. I separated the mother duck from her babies and cornered the little ducklings at a distance from the water so they couldn't escape. I reached down and scooped up one of those little fuzzy baby ducks and was so proud of myself until I turned around.

The first thing I saw was that mother duck, about twenty feet away, take flight while quacking angrily as she made a beeline directly at me like a guided missile. Like a kamikaze pilot, she flew directly into my chest, knocked me off my feet, and I landed flat on my back. I, of course, released the baby duck as my dad laughed and calmly said, "Son, I told you not to mess with those baby ducks." Wisdom is justified of her children and that event was born of foolishness.

Our turn to launch the boat finally came, and I thought it was perfect weather to remove my T-shirt and get a suntan. Dad frowned at that idea and told me I would get a sunburn if I wasn't careful. It was a wee bit cool that day with a slight breeze on the lake which had a constant water temperature of about forty-five degrees. Once we arrived at the area on the lake where Dad preferred to fish, he dropped anchor and pulled the tab from a can of Budweiser. His knowledge of fishing was vast, and I tried to pay attention when he showed me how to tie certain knots on the hooks and what bait was used for different types of fish. On that day, we were fishing for rainbow trout. Dad consistently caught more fish than I did, even though I always told him that this was the day I would skunk him. My problem was that I would get bored if I wasn't catching fish and would get distracted, and the fish would eat the bait right off the hook. He told me the second I saw that fishing line move, I needed to pull the rod toward me and set the hook in the fish's mouth. If I didn't pay attention, they would continue to steal my bait. At that age, I must have had the attention span of an otter, a mere two seconds.

During this time, Dad had guzzled several beers and needed to relieve himself. Instead of heading to the bank to take a whiz, he used his pocketknife to cut the top out of an empty beer can. He then used that can with those sharp, jagged edges as a urinal. I told him that did not look safe, and I would not be using that can. He finished uninjured, and I stood up and whizzed over the side of the boat, which I still think was the smart method. After several hours, Dad told me that I was getting very red and should put my shirt back on. He was right on both accounts because I was already sunburnt. He later told me that he was trying to help me out, recalling the instances when he was young and had made the same mistake. It was a bad burn, and my skin started peeling when we arrived home the next day.

One beautiful Indian summer day in November, we had just finished cutting firewood and had added an abundance of small limbs and brush to the already large brush pile. This brush pile was the result of many Saturdays worth of cutting firewood and was getting way too big and needed to be burned. Normally, one would pour diesel fuel on the brush pile and light it. Diesel fuel was not near as volatile as gasoline. Dad's idea was to apply a quart of the gasoline that we used to power our chainsaws onto the pile of limbs. I was suspicious from the get-go about this project and how it would end. I was told by

Dad to stand at a distance while he doused the brush pile with gasoline. One could clearly see the wet area where the gasoline had been poured. He crumpled up a newspaper and lit one end of it and crept up next to the pile, threw the newspaper toward the wet area of gas and ran back fifty feet to where I was waiting. It landed several feet below the wet area of gas, and nothing happened. We stood there for a minute waiting for the gas to ignite and still, nothing happened. The newspaper was burning but wasn't close enough to the gas to ignite it.

Dad grew impatient and started a cautious, low and determined approach to the brush pile. He was going to grab the lit newspaper and toss it up into the gasoline. He crept up, as I stood at a distance and watched while saying to myself, "This will not end well." He inched closer, and, as he was about to touch the newspaper, the earth-shaking *kaboom!* erupted. That quart of gasoline created quite an explosion with a huge burst of flames. Dad, white as a ghost, hurried back to where I stood. The explosion caught him off guard, and I was amazed he was still in one piece. He had no eyebrows or eyelashes left, and the hair on his head was singed in the front. Burnt hair was not a pleasant aroma. I said to him, "You would have kicked my butt for doing something like that." He told me that I was right and not to do as he did but do what I was told to do. How thankful I was that he didn't make me light the brush pile.

On a side note, when I was nine years old, I made use of our three-gallon gas can while I burned ants. I would douse the ant mound with gas and then light it. I accidentally caught the can on fire and somehow extinguished it before it blew me sky high. Someone has always been looking out for me, but I wouldn't know who until after I turned eighteen.

On another Saturday, we were going to haul off all the large, green trash bags that were piling up next to our fruit cellar in the backyard. We had a new ravine—like the one from when we lived in the woods—located on the west side of the farm. After Dad and I had loaded about six bags of trash into the bed of the truck, we noticed a large rat that ran and hid under the remaining trash bags still on the ground. Dad told me to run to the shed and get the three tined pitchfork so that he could kill that rat. I returned from the shed and gave the pitchfork to him, and he told me to slowly pick up each bag, and he would be ready to skewer that nasty creature when he appeared.

Each bag I picked up caused that rat to run and hide under whatever bags remained on the ground. We were down to the last bag. With nowhere left to hide, our pet was going to have to make a break for it, and Dad was ready. So far Dad's plan has been going great. What could possibly go wrong? Dad readied himself, in position to harpoon that rat with his pitchfork as I slowly raised the last bag; the rat was now uncovered and unprotected. That rodent just stood there motionless and confused with nowhere to hide. Dad gave his all as he attempted to spear that vermin. He stuck the pitchfork directly over the rat and into the ground. Unfortunately for Dad, the rat was between the tines of the pitchfork and uninjured.

Mr. Rat leaped onto my dad's pant leg and held on for dear life. Screaming came forth from my father that would have made you think he'd just fallen out of an airplane with no parachute! I had never heard my sisters cry out in such a fashion. His accompanying dance moves would have made any choreographer extremely proud. The dance and the screams were hysterical. That rat had a death grip on his pant leg, and it took some fancy moves on Dad's part to shake him loose. I had no weapon, so I was of no use to him in his time of need and just stood there and watched as it all played out. I am not sure who was more afraid of whom, Dad or the rat. We didn't kill that rat because once Dad shook it free from his leg, it ran off and was never seen again. I knew better than to make any wise cracks to him, so I just shook my head and laughed. Apples don't fall far from the tree, and I realized that I was more like my father than I cared to admit!

27

Own Worst Enemy

On a warm day in June, my mom was going shopping in a nearby town. She informed my two younger sisters and me that we were required to go. Helga was always in trouble at home and constantly caused problems for herself and those closest to her. She lived in crisis mode and brought most of her tribulations upon herself. Hearing that her presence was required on this shopping trip, Helga unleashed her typical rant of whining and crying in an attempt to get out of going. Mom was not agreeable to any of it. Helga was twelve and acted as if she was four years old. She told Mom explicitly that she was not going.

Dad's words of wisdom flashed through my mind. *Kick your brain in gear before opening your mouth.* I have found that to be very sound advice. Helga missed out on that memo and was continually putting her foot in her mouth. She was determined to do things her way whether right or wrong. Her idiotic behavior has cost her dearly over the years, but that has not discouraged her the least bit. She was a glutton for punishment. Mom got the three of us loaded into the car, and I called shotgun since I was the oldest sibling. That left Helga and Monica in the backseat, and Helga continued her nonstop complaining. The rest of us were sick of listening to her drivel on and on.

We pulled out of our driveway onto the gravel county road, and Helga flipped out, flung open the backdoor of the car, and proceeded to jump to freedom. Or so she imagined. Fortunately for her, she realized at the last second what a stupid idea that was and hung on to the rear door as she and the door swung out over the gravel road at twenty miles per hour. She put her feet down on the gravel and was doing what we later termed, "Gravel Skiing" while she maintained a death grip on the backdoor of the vehicle. She was screaming for Mom to stop the car as Monica, and I watched in disbelief. Helga's eyes were as big as silver dollars while gravel skiing. Mom stopped the car and, like it or not, Helga was spanked immediately. She still had to go to town with us in spite of all the whining and foolish behavior. As always, she accomplished nothing by her ridiculous behavior, although it was very entertaining to witness.

In another instance, Helga wanted to go to town with some friends, and Dad denied her request. She threw a conniption fit. He told her she was not going to talk to him like that and her sassy mouth would get her a spanking. She was twelve and yelled at Dad that he was not going to spank her, then called him a *mother fu$#&r* as she ran into the standing cornfield next to our house. Dad yelled into the cornfield, "When it gets dark, you will come crawling back home and there will be a spanking waiting for you!"

I am still bewildered as to why Dad thought it was a good idea to get his shotgun and shoot it above the cornfield so that birdshot rained down into the stalks of corn. He did it to scare Helga, and it worked because she thought he was shooting directly at her. I concluded that at least two of my family members had lost their minds. I laid low the rest of the afternoon and eagerly awaited the blowup that would take place after dark (Helga's spanking).

Sure enough, at sunset, darkness enveloped the field, and she came skulking out, knowing the gallows awaited her. Dad was waiting, and I was waiting because I was sure calling Dad a *mother fu$#&r* guaranteed the use of capital punishment. Dad laid hold of her, and with each lash of his thin leather belt, curse words spewed from her mouth! The more she cussed him out, the more swats she received. The quickest way out of a hole that you've dug for yourself is to first stop digging deeper. Helga continued digging deeper and deeper until her latest stunt ended with her being grounded for two weeks and all those swats to boot. Experience is a wonderful tutor, but you need to pay attention!

I remember when I was thirteen and smarted off to my mom, not cursing her but just being a smart aleck, while she was dusting the living room. She held a large can of Lemon Pledge in one hand and her dust cloth in the other. No sooner than those sassy words left my smart mouth, she side-armed that can of Lemon Pledge across the living room and directly into my forehead. It hurt and I started to cry! She nailed me with that can because of my smart mouth and felt horrible for doing it. This was way out of the ordinary for her behavior. She was always so sweet and tender, but I pushed her to the limit and was never that rude to her again. I feared and respected both of my parents, especially Dad for obvious reasons. I never spoke to either of my parents with the bitterly harsh words that Helga ranted. I don't think she ever learned from that experience.

As Helga advanced into her teen years, she regularly snuck out of the house at night to be with her friends. She waited until everyone was in bed and crept out the girls' bedroom window, onto the front porch, and then climbed down the ladder she had placed there earlier that evening. She then walked to the end of our drive where her friends picked her up and headed to town. She got by with this on many nights until she forgot to put the ladder up just once. Dad saw the ladder leaning against the front porch and immediately knew someone had been sneaking out at night. Cameron was not going to take the rap, so she told Dad that Helga was the guilty party. Helga was grounded for two weeks, and Dad, from that point on, made regular inspections of the exterior of the house before he went to bed.

I never snuck out at night but broke my curfew on plenty of occasions. I had a midnight curfew on weekends after I turned sixteen, and it was difficult to arrive late and sneak up to bed without Dad knowing. One such night, I pulled into our driveway at one o'clock in super stealth mode without headlights and shut off the truck as I coasted the last little bit up our drive. I had been drinking beer and was in no condition for a confrontation with Dad. Once parked, I sat in the truck with my head resting on the steering wheel. Someone started knocking on the truck window. Thank heavens, it was my mom! She asked me if I had been drinking, and I said no, an obvious lie. She told me that I had better get in the house and get to bed before Dad woke up. She must have smelled the beer on me but said nothing. Mom was pretty good about cutting you some slack, even though you for sure didn't deserve any.

28

Carrot Top

I could pen an entire book about my older, redheaded brother, Archie. I liked him best of all my brothers; his entertainment through the years added spice to my childhood. In grade school, he was given an assignment to write a poem, and below is what he told me that he wrote. I am hopeful he did not borrow this from another author. Here is the poem:

I saw a birdie lying in the snow,

He was hurt you know.

I lured him close with a crust of bread,

And then I stomped that birdie's head.

What could I say? I thought it was really funny, and Archie was usually going for a laugh. He was always scads of fun if Dad didn't find out what we were up to.

Archie had a taste for the firewater and followed in Dad's footsteps. My dad's drinking got so bad when he was in his mid-fifties that it almost killed him. He was mixing bourbon with prescription meds that he received from his dentist for tooth pain. The drugs and alcohol took their toll and put Dad in the hospital for over a week. He even tried to sneak a fifth of Johnny Walker Red Label into the hospital when checking in. The nurses found it tucked away in his suitcase, and at that point, Dad was officially off the booze. When he was released from the hospital, he was ready to get back to church and start living the right way. Before that episode, we had been unchurched for five or more years which had a negative effect on each of us. Vernie refused to return to church with the rest of us and never attended again.

Archie, at age eighteen, was always coming home drunk and did a decent job of concealing it from Dad. Many late nights, he coasted the car up our driveway with the headlights off, hoping Dad was in bed and sound asleep. His next feat was to climb onto the roof of our back porch and walk across the roof up to the second-story window above the front porch that entered the boys' bedroom. Three of us boys slept in that room on bunkbeds. Each time Archie stomped across the roof late at night, I thought I heard thunder. I grew accustomed to seeing a dark figure sneaking through our bedroom window late at night on weekends. We had a second window in our bedroom that Archie often used as a urinal. Our only bathroom was downstairs, and you had to walk through my parents' bedroom to get to it. I was awakened on many a late night to the sound of liquid spraying through the window screen of our bedroom, and it was usually Archie after a big night of drinking. Vernie and I decided to avail ourselves of this extremely convenient urinal. Mom had her suspicions as to how that window screen became so rusty and often questioned us as to why none of the other screens were discolored. Archie convinced her that it must be exposed to more rain than the other screens. He was an amazing brother!

Living at Green Acres was a bona fide challenge on several fronts. All six of us siblings slept in the two bedrooms upstairs, and it was blazing hot in the summertime. Dad installed an air conditioning window unit in the living room downstairs which did absolutely nothing for the people upstairs. He would complain because we opened the windows in our bedrooms and had fans blowing the less hot air from outside into our rooms. It was a hopeless attempt at surviving the heatwave located on the top floor. That combined with the noise from the hogs constantly clanging the feeder lids made for many a restless night. Countless nights, I wouldn't get to sleep until it cooled down, and that might be three o'clock in the morning.

Archie started growing his hair long, and Vernie and I thought that was pretty cool and started letting our hair grow long too. Dad did not like the hippie look and was not shy about sharing his opinions. He was opposed to the long hair and hippie sandals that Vernie and Archie wore. Dad was opinionated, much like the character Archie Bunker on the TV show "All in The Family."

Another time, Archie and Vernie had just purchased some new leather sandals that Dad did not approve of. Large brass rings adorned the top of both pairs of sandals, and we thought they were totally hip. Dad did not see the coolness in their latest purchase and viewed those sandals as another step taken by his sons into hippiedom. He was determined to stop that progression and save his sons from becoming full-on hippies. He threw a fit about those new shoes and took both pairs out into our gravel driveway, poured gasoline on them, and lit them up. Archie's and Vernie's complaints fell on deaf ears as flames consumed their new slippers. When the fire died down, I went out and dug the brass rings out of the ashes and kept them for souvenirs. Things were crazy that day. I think Dad had been into the firewater, or calmer heads would have prevailed.

When Archie was in his first year of college, he and a friend were out late one Friday night drinking beer and he either fell asleep or passed out while driving his Volkswagen Beetle. He crashed head-on into a telephone pole. Archie's voice box and esophagus were crushed from his impact against the steering wheel. He would have suffocated to death if it weren't for the fast-thinking state trooper who arrived on the scene and performed an emergency tracheotomy on him. The trooper cut open Archie's throat and inserted a small tube into his esophagus so that he could breathe. He was rushed to the hospital for surgery and spent more than a week there. He had also broken his nose—for the second time in his life.

When he finally came home from the hospital, his face was still so bruised and discolored that the younger siblings would cry at the sight of him. They ran from him screaming as if he were a monster. He had a trachea tube in the front of his neck for many months, and his voice from that point on was so raspy, he sounded like Clint Eastwood when he spoke.

Archie endured many more surgeries after that in an attempt to keep the scar tissue from building up in his throat and hopefully give him a stronger voice. It was more of a raspy whisper than a voice. I doubt it was any benefit that Archie was a smoker and continued to smoke after the crash. For him to smoke a cigarette, he put the cigarette to his mouth and used his index finger to cover the hole in the trachea tube so he could draw in smoke. Then he blew the smoke out of the trachea tube and totally grossed us out. At other times, in order to mess with his younger siblings, he put the lit cigarette directly into his trachea tube and drew in smoke and again blew it back out through the tube. It was all so disturbing, and he loved to use his newly acquired talents to entertain us.

The worst part of all was when he would use the small vacuum that the hospital sent home with him. He would insert a small rubber tube into his trachea tube that was connected to the vac unit. This was used to suck out the phlegm and whatever else was in his scarred-up throat. This yucky stuff was deposited into a clear glass bottle next to the vacuum. This process made an awful sucking, slurping sound as he coughed repeatedly, and the slime was removed from his throat. The added bonus? Being able to see it all in that clear glass jar. Archie always made a dramatic event out of that disgusting daily routine, and of course I was always there to observe. He has never fully recovered from his injuries but has lived a very productive life despite everything this world has thrown at him.

29

Baseball Career

My baseball career began in Little League at age twelve. After attending a week's worth of baseball camp, I was ready to make my mark in the arena of sports. My baseball skills, however, had improved very little. I was always small for my age and didn't have the experience required to improve my skills.

Another kid my age, and about the same size, was playing second base during a Little League game. It was obvious from what happened next that he didn't know the proper way to guard second base. He positioned himself wrong when he put his left leg between the base and the runner. He paid dearly for that mistake. The base runner was trying to steal second, so the catcher threw the ball to the second baseman in an attempt to tag the runner out. It was going to be a close play, and the runner thought it best to slide into second. He slid directly into the second baseman's leg that was trapped between the base and the sliding runner. With his foot pinned against the bag, the impact snapped his leg just above the ankle with a loud *POP!* that all the other players heard loud and clear. He screamed hysterically from pain. His leg was snapped in two and doubled over. Coach picked him up to carry him to the car, and his foot flopped in the breeze. What a gruesome sight! I never knew baseball could be so dangerous. He recovered, but his baseball career was never the same after that accident. From that day on, I carried in my pocket what I thought was a lucky rabbit's foot to each baseball game for protection.

My baseball career ending injury happened one evening as my dad and oldest brother, Leroy, watched. Leroy was home from college, and I wanted to skip my game and spend some time with him. Dad vetoed that because the team needed me. I wasn't a very good player, so I found it difficult to believe they wouldn't do just fine without me. That little voice inside my head was telling me to skip this game, but Dad insisted that I attend. When the game started, I, of course, was at the bottom of the batting lineup because the other players on my team outperformed me. Anticipating my turn at bat, I watched as player after player on my team produced base hits off the pitcher. The pitcher didn't throw very fast, but he was accurate and easy to get a hit from. I couldn't wait to get my shot at batting because I knew I could hit the ball at that speed. When my turn came to bat, they replaced the easy pitcher with a kid who looked big enough to play high school baseball.

The new pitcher threw extremely fast and was not at all accurate. My only hope was to stand there and maybe get a walk out of it. This happened often, and I counted on it again. As I stood there, watching him warm up, the ball was traveling so fast that it made a whizzing sound as it passed through the air. To say that I was nervous would have been an understatement. Then the umpire shouted, "Batter up!" I stepped to the plate with high hopes of maybe impressing my dad and brother with a base hit. The first pitch came zipping in at a high rate of speed. Too high, so ball one. I would have been perfectly happy with a walk at that point and being short gave me the advantage of having a small strike zone. The second pitch came slicing through the air and directly at my head. I attempted to get out of the way but wasn't quick enough. That rock-hard baseball hit me squarely in my left eye, traveling at who knows how fast. It drove me into the dirt!

When I came to, my coach, dad, brother, and a bunch of other people stood over me, staring in disbelief as to what just took place. People asked me if I was all right. In a stupor, I was for sure, *not* all right. The area around my left eye became so swollen that I couldn't see from that eye. It turned black and blue and green and remained swollen for weeks. The worst part of it was that I was now afraid of the ball while batting. I would constantly back away from home plate after a pitch was thrown, thinking I was going to be pummeled again. I was no good at batting from then on. Eventually, I gave up baseball and often reminded Dad that he should have let me skip that game. That so-called lucky rabbit's foot I carried in my pocket was thrown into a box in my closet and never trusted again.

30

Hey Rod

Archie's good friend, Rod, was a frequent guest at our home located on the hog farm in the 1970s. Rod, a happy individual, liked to joke around, and that was all the incentive I needed to hide and attempt to scare him each time he arrived at our residence. I was twelve when Rod first started coming around, and oftentimes he brought his girlfriend with him. They both laughed at the silly things I did and spoke. My main goal was to get a few laughs out of them.

Those games went on for about a month, and I got pretty good at watching for Rod's arrival and getting into my hiding position before he parked in our drive. I wasn't sure why Archie addressed him as, "Hey Rod" and other people referred to Rod in that same manner. Maybe his first name was Hey? Anyway, I had found an excellent hiding spot next to our steps at the backdoor, and when Rod was in range, I jumped out and really caught him off guard that time. He yelled, "Billy Weird!" and the nickname stuck. That was what Hey Rod called me from then on. He enjoyed placing emphasis on the word *Weird* when he addressed me by that name.

Looking back on all the hysterical laughter my many antics produced, I can't help but assume my brother and Hey Rod were smoking some left-handed cigarettes for them to be so overtly susceptible to my silliness. They would laugh uncontrollably until tears were streaming from their eyes. I was either a polished comedian, or they were smoking weed. Either way, I had fun toying with their minds with my comedic behavior. I later found out that his name was A. Rod!

31

Mom's Quail

I turned fifteen in 1973 and was still just a kid waiting to grow up. My bicycle was still my main form of transportation unless I could bum a ride from an older sibling or friend.

Cameron had high hopes of convincing Dad to allow her to borrow his truck so she could head into town and cruise around one afternoon. I don't remember what excuse she used, but Dad wasn't going to let her go by herself. He told her that she could go if she took her younger brother, Billy (that's me). She reluctantly said yes, and we both jumped into Dad's pickup and headed into town for the afternoon. I was thrilled, and this excursion would introduce me to a new form of entertainment. Whenever our father did let us go to town, we enjoyed cruising Main Street, and if there was no activity in our town, we headed to one of the other small towns in the area and motored around. There were also two county seats in close proximity to where we lived, and they both had a courthouse with a surrounding square on which to tool around.

On this day, we didn't need to leave our little burg because we met up with Brandon, a classmate of my sister's, and got into his car to cruise around. Dad was never happy with all the meandering, putting miles on his truck, and burning through his gasoline. He always told his friends he didn't need to put antifreeze in his vehicles because, with so many teenagers driving, the cars never sat long enough to cool off. We tried to switch cars and ride at least part of the time with others so Dad didn't have a fit about all the miles being put on his truck. Brandon was happy to have us galivant around with him.

Not long after we were seated in his car, Brandon asked Cameron if I was cool. She turned around and looked at me from the front seat and said, "Yeah, he's cool." Not sure how cool I was but couldn't wait to find out! Brandon pulled a joint out of his shirt pocket and asked if we wanted to smoke some. Cameron immediately said yes, and I learned that she was no stranger to smoking weed. I said yes, and that was my first-time smoking. Brandon lit it up, and we passed it around and each took several puffs. I coughed uncontrollably after each puff. The two of them laughed at me as I gagged on each drag from the doobie. They both kept asking me if I felt anything, and I said no. I was still feeling nothing as we said our good-byes to Brandon and headed back home.

Upon arriving at home, we noticed that Dad was gone in Mom's car, and Mom was in the kitchen reading through a recipe for dinner. Cameron and I sat down at the dinner table with Mom; I still felt nothing from our puffs of marijuana. Mom started telling us a story about a quail she had seen earlier in the front yard. She was so theatrical in her description, acting out how the quail darted across the yard a short distance and then poked his head up high to see around, then he crouched back down, darted a little bit farther, and raised his head again to peer around.

Witnessing Mom's impersonation of this small bird was high comedy! Cameron and I both lost it and were laughing uncontrollably as tears streamed from our eyes. This just spurred Mom on with her story. The more she told us about the quail and laughed at us laughing, the more we all laughed. I definitely felt something now and just needed the right catalyst to get me there, and Mom's story was sending me to the moon. She never even suspected that Cameron and I had just smoked marijuana. Mom was such a sweet woman and not well versed in the ways of the world. Dad, on the other hand, would not put anything past any of us. That was the first time I ever smoked weed and would not be the last!

32

High School

Being from a small school, I was in the same building as the high school students when I went into seventh grade. I was always short for my age and the runt of my brothers. Being in the high school building made me feel puny while around the older pupils.

My eighth-grade history teacher was a pervert! History class was not a class that I looked forward to at all. The other boys in my class dreaded it just as much as I did. We referred to the teacher as Mr. Cesspool for obvious reasons. If you were a boy, you did not want to ask any questions in class because Mr. Cesspool thought it was an open invitation to come and squat down next to your desk and discreetly place his hand between your legs while thumping your crotch with his thumb. When that happened to me, I hollered loud enough that the whole class could hear me, "Stop it!" Getting the attention of the whole class would make him stop. The other boys in the class did the same thing.

That guy was a real sicko, and from the way he smelled, I don't believe he was very familiar with soap and water. I even told some of the other teachers what he was doing, but they thought I was making it up. Fortunately, he was gone the next year, and I didn't have to deal with that again. Mr. Cesspool was also a Boy Scout leader. Thanks to being a bedwetter, I was never a Boy Scout because I didn't want to have an accident on a campout. When I found out from the other guys at school what went on at the campouts, I was forever thankful that I did not participate. They told me that Mr. Cesspool was forever trying to get several of the boys to sleep in his tent and was continually trying to get into their underwear! As far as I know, none of the kids let him do what he wanted, but some might have been too ashamed to talk about what had happened.

That same year, a male science teacher was having sex with one of the senior girls. She spoke freely about their relationship, and that teacher was not back at school the next year because the school board found out about it. Anyone who says that small schools are boring has obviously not attended one.

Vernie continued to make my life miserable until I was around thirteen. When I was twelve, I bought two, twenty-five-pound dumbbells and worked out with them several times a day. My parents even noticed and commented on how my muscles were growing, and Vernie hated hearing any compliments coming my way. He was never interested in putting in the work that it took to build yourself up, and as a result, he remained skinny. He was taller than me, which intimidated me; therefore, I never fought back because I would get pummeled even worse. After working out with weights for a year or so, I was really getting beefed up for a thirteen-year-old. One afternoon, Vernie cornered me on the back porch of our house and started the usual shoving me around as he was bigger. Out of nowhere, I punched him as hard as I could right in the stomach which caught him off guard and knocked the wind out of him. I took off running, fearing for my life, but that time he did not pursue me. As a matter of fact, he never treated me like that again. He would still say mean things to me, but the physical abuse was over. It is amazing what a little respect will do!

More interested in mischief and being funny, I enjoyed the social aspects of attending school, though I did not like the studies. I was totally awful when we had a substitute teacher. It was my calling to be the funny guy or the one up to no good. My first substitute teacher victim was when I was in eighth grade English class. She was a nice enough lady and fresh out of college with dreams and ideals that just sparkled with enthusiasm, and I wanted no part of it. Miss English was to be our sub for the week, and her first day did not go as she had anticipated because of little old me.

On her first day, I sat in the back of the classroom so that none of the real students could see what I was up to and perhaps rat me out to the principal. When Miss English was writing at the chalkboard in the front of the room with her back toward the class, I took the gum from my mouth and threw it in her general direction. Unfortunately for her, it landed in the back of her hair. She felt the impact and asked who did that. When nobody fessed up, she started to cry when she felt the gum that was stuck firmly in her hair. I was not proficient at baseball, so my aim was way off. My objective was to zero in on the blackboard, and I felt bad when the gum adhered to her hair. I was always a prime suspect but was never brought up on charges for that one.

My freshman year, the math teacher was on maternity leave. Our substitute was an odd-looking, strange-acting lady who none of the class was enamored with. On her second day of teaching, I entered the classroom, walked past the chalkboard, grabbed an eraser from the tray, and headed to my seat in the back of the room. I didn't permit anyone to see that I had copped an eraser. When the sub's back was turned and she was writing out our lesson with chalk, I threw the eraser, and it smacked the blackboard right next to her head. She turned around and angrily asked, "Who threw that?" She was furious! I probably had guilt written all over my face, but I had positioned myself so as not to make eye contact with her. Nobody knew who threw the eraser, so nobody was punished. Thankfully, I finally outgrew that sort of behavior. I did, however, evolve into other areas of misconduct. My life was a steady, downward spiral from which I could not escape.

Early in my sophomore year, a kid named Bobby brought a bag of pills to school one Friday morning and began passing them out to anyone interested. He told each of us that they were tranquilizers for the criminally insane. Myself and about ten other students took one each, Helga included. Everything was hunky-dory until about the midway point of first period. I became so groggy that I barely made it to my second-hour class. I laid my head on my desk throughout second period, and when the bell rang, I sluggishly made my way to the office to tell them that I was sick and ought to go home.

It was a great plan for someone so out of it except for the fact that when I arrived at the office, several students were already there with the same idea. Everyone who took one of those pills ended up in the office, and the office quickly figured out that something was awry. One of the guilty students told the principal what had taken place, and the police were promptly called. Helga denied any involvement in this episode and never admitted that she took a pill. She said that she was genuinely ill. I fessed up and just wanted to go home and sleep, and sleep I did for the next eighteen hours. The student who brought the pills to school found himself in serious trouble with the police, and I was not sure how that turned out for him. He never returned to school, and the story going around was that he was sent to a boys' home because that was not his first offense.

My buddy, Arnold, was not a good influence on me, and I am sure I wasn't a good influence on him either. Which meant when we were together, trouble was just over the next hill. When Arnold was around my parents, he was always on his best behavior and said, "Yes, sir," and "Yes, ma'am," and was way too polite. He liked to brag to me that he had my parents eating out of his hand, and they in turn thought he was such a nice boy. He for sure had the wool pulled over their eyes.

One Saturday in the summer of 1975, Arnold had purchased two hits of what he called the *yellow microdot*. I had never heard of such a thing, and he told me it was LSD and offered me one of the tiny, round yellow pills. That was all new to me, so I said, "Sure, I'll try one." We each took a hit, and I waited to see what it would do to me. After thirty minutes or so, a pleasurable rush overcame me, similar to a shiver when you are cold. I received a rush about every twenty minutes and each one became more intense and more frequent as the day went on. As the shivers became more enhanced, they propelled me into outbursts of uncontrollable laughter. We thought it would be a good idea to get wherever we were going before that stuff really kicked in and affected our ability to drive the car.

Arnold drove to a small town to the south of us as we listened to "Dream Weaver" by Gary Wright and many other 70s Rock hits playing on the radio. We parked on the square and went into the local recreation center which was a real hole-in-the-wall. Courtney, a girl we saw in the recreation center, was tall and skinny with flaming red hair. She strolled up where we were seated and started chatting with us. That was the point when the hallucinations started. In my messed-up mind, she morphed into a giant, red-haired rabbit, and I laughed uncontrollably as I gawked at her. I told Arnold that she looked like a rabbit, and he burst into frenzied laughter along with me. Courtney did not know that we had taken LSD, and she was upset that we were laughing at her. We could not control our outbursts and had drawn way too much attention from everyone else in the recreation center.

We left that town and headed back to Arnold's house, knowing that no one would be at home there. His mind was so jumbled that he ordered me to drive the car, and I was so warped that I said sure, and away we went. I drove on the highway at forty-five miles per hour, and it felt as though the car floated down the road like a spacecraft. As we topped each hill, we simultaneously let out a yell, like we were riding on a roller coaster, but we were only traveling forty-five miles per hour. Arnold kept asking me how fast I was driving and continued to tell me to slow down. Other drivers passed us and honked their horns while directing some all too familiar hand gestures our way. I was hallucinating so intensely that the highway itself appeared to be moving like a wide, flat ribbon blowing in the breeze as we floated on top of it to our next destination. It was like playing Mario Kart while driving on rainbow road.

Somehow, we arrived safe and sound—well, maybe not sound—to Arnold's house and sat outside on his lawn. When the grass blew in the breeze, it took on a life of its own, and I couldn't tell what was stationary and what was in motion. I moved my hand in front of my face, and it would leave tracers, which meant I saw a dozen or so images of my hand long after my hand was no longer in front of my face. The rushes became more and more intense, lasting five to six hours, and I was ready for it to stop. How many hours can one laugh and still enjoy it? When I lay down in my bed that night and closed my eyes, all I could see was a paisley print. I am almost certain the person who came up with that design was tripping on acid.

The next day after my first trip on LSD, I told Arnold, "Don't you ever give me any of that stuff again!" The aftereffects were awful, and I sunk into depression for several days afterward. It was like I had used up all my happiness in those six hours of extreme exuberance. Time makes us forget the bad things, and because of that Arnold talked me into doing LSD two more times that summer. I have not touched that stuff since and have no intention of doing so in the future.

33

Ella

Ella was my first long-term girlfriend. I was fifteen and she was seventeen. She was in Cameron's class, and they were both cheerleaders. I was attracted to Ella but wasn't sure if she was interested in me. I was on the varsity basketball team my sophomore year because at our small school, they had to bump me up from B team to A team so the A team would have enough players. It wasn't because I was a basketball phenom. They needed a warm body to warm the bench. I was a sophomore and got to ride the bus to away games with the juniors and seniors. Was I cool or what?

Coming home from one of our away games, we were all singing whatever anyone had a hankering to sing. We were belting out songs about people in love and inserting the names of couples into the songs. Cameron started singing Billy and Ella, and the whole bus joined in. I just happened to be in a seat directly across the aisle from Ella. We were not yet a couple, but things were about to change. Cameron started yelling for Ella and me to kiss, and the entire bus started chanting for the kiss. So, we kissed and kissed, and after about a minute of kissing, there was an array of cheers and applause. That was the beginning of our nearly two-year relationship!

Immediately after our first kiss, Ella and I were an item and insepa-rable. She possessed a driver's license, and my social life was expand-ing by leaps and bounds. Ella would borrow her mom's big Ford sta-tion wagon and pick me up for dates. We kissed and kissed and made anyone and everyone sick to their stomach who had to be around us during these kissing marathons. Ella was dropping me off at my house one evening, and her younger sister, who was my age, was in the car with us. We parked in my driveway, and it was time for the kiss goodbye. I remember "Crocodile Rock" by Elton John was one of the songs playing on the radio as we kissed and kissed. Her sister grew so tired of all the slurping and smacking that she said, "Please stop and take me home." After a few more slurps of affection, we called it quits for the night, and she and her sister headed home.

Ella's senior prom was coming up, and lo and behold, she asked me to attend the evening's festivities with her. Our school was all abuzz with the junior/senior prom fast approaching. Sophomores were not usually involved with the setup and decorating, but the juniors and seniors needed some extra help, so Arnold and I volunteered to get out of class. By design, they sent Arnold and me to do the dangerous work up in the gymnasium attic. We didn't care; we just wanted to be out of class. Our task was to place a layer of colored cellophane over several of the lights located in the gym ceiling. We made our way to the attic and learned what all the fuss was about and why they couldn't send just anybody up there to complete that project. The attic had some two-by-twelve wooden planks positioned across the top of the ceiling joists to use for walking paths. If you acciden-tally stepped between the ceiling joists, you could fall through the gym ceiling and onto the gymnasium floor about thirty feet below. Not a good option!

Arnold thought we should smoke some weed while we were in the attic with no supervision, and that's exactly what we did. After smoking, we started moving from light to light with the colored cellophane, making some real progress toward finishing. I felt so confident—after having completed several of the lights and walking on the two-by-twelve walk boards—that I could simply walk on top of the ceiling joists and maybe finish the project sooner than later. Arnold was cutting cellophane and getting it ready to cover the next light. I took off walking across the top of the joists and tripped and fell between two of them. My legs and lower body busted through the gym ceiling, sending several of the two-by-four-foot ceiling tiles that were nailed to the bottom of the joists crashing to the gym floor.

Fortunately for me, I caught myself by my elbows and held on to the joists for dear life. Students were screaming and panicking below as my buddy calmly looked over at me and said, "Billy, you are such an idiot." He did nothing, made no attempt to come over and help me. I pulled the lower half of my body back up into the attic and was much more cautious when decorating the remaining lights. After we finished our task, we headed to math class, and the teacher declared as we walked into the room, "We all know what Billy and Arnold have been up too!" I figured she smelled the weed on us. That was the same math teacher who told me that if I would apply myself just a little in her class, she wouldn't flunk me. I must have tried a little because I somehow received a passing grade in her class.

Prom with Ella was amazing; we had a good time. She picked me up in her mother's Ford station wagon. We were traveling in style. Loads of socializing and dancing took place, and we ended the night by finding a nice, secluded gravel road out in the middle of nowhere on which to park and get to know one another even better. One thing led to another, and I became a man that night!

Within a few days of becoming a man, my crotch started itching with a vengeance! I found a small creature in my underwear and did not know what it was. I asked Cameron and described to her the small insect, and she said I probably had crab lice. I couldn't believe it! Walls in public restrooms held signs that read, "Don't even bother to wipe the seat, because the Arkansas Crabs can jump ten feet." I always wiped the seat, and I still got crabs. Cameron told me that our whole family could be infested with crab lice if I didn't get rid of them soon. They can be spread from one person to another from a toilet seat. Helga and Vernie could enjoy them for a spell, but I certainly didn't want my parents getting crabs because of me. I talked to Ella, and it turned out her former boyfriend was cheating on her and that was why she ended it with him. Unfortunately, she didn't realize he had left her with a little going away present that she unknowingly shared with me. I got crab lice the first time that I had sex, and it didn't slow me down in the least. Ella and I bought some shampoo to kill the invaders, and it worked great. Our little "friends" were all gone and no one else in my house was the wiser. That was a first and a last for me, and I never needed that shampoo again.

Arnold and I hung out quite a bit together, and Ella accompanied us on several of our misadventures. One such night, we were all three drinking some wine and were extra giddy when someone suggested that we all strip off our clothes and drive to the nearest town naked. We stripped off and were riding in my dad's pickup, listening to the Rolling Stones on the radio as we traveled at ninety miles per hour toward the next town. That would have been something if a state trooper had stopped us, and we were all in our birthday suits! My dad and the local state trooper were fishing buddies, so that would have been really fun explaining to Dad what I was thinking. We made it just fine to the next town and got dressed. Arnold, after seeing my girlfriend naked, started calling her and trying to get her to go out with him. She refused, but he continued to call.

Several individuals were jealous that I had a girlfriend, and they had absolutely no prospects in the foreseeable future. Vernie was jealous because he was nineteen and still had no girlfriend. He even threatened to tell Mom and Dad about Ella and I and our night moves. Thankfully he kept quiet and left our relationship in our hands. He enjoyed having us cruise around town with him so that he didn't have to be alone. If I had a dollar for every mile that Vernie cruised around in his car, I would be a multi-millionaire. He was known in our small community as the night hawk because he was always out cruising late into the night while drinking beer.

One snowy evening, Vernie, Ella, and I were out tooling around in Vernie's 1958 Chevy while it was snowing like crazy. The big, fluffy snowflakes were hypnotic as we watched them floating in front of the headlights of the car while we drove down a blacktop highway near our town. We smoked some weed and drank a couple of beers and were having a fun time. Snow covered the roads at a rapid rate, so Vernie thought it best to slow down a bit. When he applied the brakes, his '58 Chevy decided to do a 180. At the same time, all three of us looked backward over the front seat because we were now traveling in reverse going about fifty miles per hour. I distinctly remember the song "The Joker" by the Steve Miller Band played on the eight-track as Vernie did a great job driving backward at that speed until his car decided to turn around and go forward. This time, Vernie couldn't keep the car on the road; it spun around, and the backend went into the ditch and jabbed the rear driver's side into the ditch embankment. We shot back out onto the road, miraculously headed in the proper direction. All three of us let out a scream but were very pleased with the outcome. Vernie had some minor damage to his car, but it was not enough to slow us down, and we completed our night of revelry.

There were other older guys at school who didn't like the fact that I had a girlfriend, and they didn't. Thomas was running his mouth to several people and saying that my girlfriend was a tramp. Arnold overheard what was said and told me that I needed to put a stop to his big mouth. Arnold had been taunting me all morning to confront Thomas, and that afternoon I finally got up the nerve to confront him. Word spread like wildfire that sparks were about to fly between the two of us. I caught up with Thomas in the hallway at school and told him he better keep his mouth shut about my girlfriend. His response was, "If you are going to do anything about it, then do it now!"

Thomas was bigger than me, as were most of the other guys, but I wasted no time in defending my girlfriend's honor. Though small, I proved to be quite a scrapper. While sporting a huge smile on my face, I used my left hand and grabbed him by the lapel of his Levi's jacket and went to work on his smart mouth with my right fist. I rapidly hit him in the face three times before he could get hold of me. By the time he grabbed me, most of the fight was gone out of him, and he was hanging on for dear life as I continued to pummel his face and head. The large class ring on my right hand made for a very formidable weapon as I landed blow after blow. The school principal broke up the fight, and when the dust cleared, I felt horrible about what I had done to him. Arnold had been pushing for that to happen all morning, and I let him have too much influence over me. I had broken Thomas's nose and damaged his sinus cavity and was filled with remorse about the whole exchange. We both received a three-day suspension, and my dad all but patted me on the back for winning a fight. He loved it when his children stood up for themselves and didn't let people use them for a doormat.

I went out for cross-country track that same year and didn't do too badly running against all the taller runners. I even took tenth place out of thirty runners in a two-mile cross-country event and was given a medal. That was the only year we had any track events at my school because our new superintendent was a runner and started the program which only lasted for the one year that he was there. Several of our practice runs were with the superintendent and some other guys, so we were all well acquainted.

On the day I received my one and only track medal, we had an all-school assembly for several awards to be given out to various students. The superintendent gave a short speech about the benefits of exercise and how running was a great way to keep fit. He called two other students from the bleachers to the center of the gym and presented them with their track medals. He then called me down to present me with my tenth-place award. I hurried from the bleachers and stood right next to him as he continued touting the virtues of being a runner. While I stood there next to him, he placed his arm around me with his hand on my shoulder and spoke of my vast improvements as a runner. To be funny and not knowing what a huge response I would receive, I laid my head on his shoulder while he still had his arm around me. The entire gymnasium burst into laughter! My sheer delight was short lived as he very forcefully squeezed my neck with his hand that had been on my shoulder. I knew that meant stop fooling around, so I lifted my head up off his shoulder as the laughter rang on. Ella later told me how funny it was to view from the bleachers.

My seventeenth birthday rolled around, and I had permission to drive my mom's 1970 Chevy Impala. I was ready to party! I had a date with Ella at seven o'clock that evening and thought it would be fun to head to Vernie's little house beforehand for a bit of smoking the ganja. I took with me a quarter of an ounce in a sandwich bag with two joints already twisted up and ready to smoke. Vernie was always a willing participant when it came to smoking some weed. When he was still living at home, I knew where his weed stash was under his bed and helped myself to it on several occasions. He questioned me a few times about taking some of his pot. What was he going to do, tell Mom and Dad that I was into his weed stash without his permission? I think not!

Arnold was always appreciative when I showed up for a night of partying with a gift from Vernie. I stopped by to see my older bro, and we puffed the magic dragon until it was time to go pick up Ella. Upon leaving Vernie's place, I quickly realized how scrambled my brain was and that I should not be driving. But there I was behind the wheel and headed south, both literally and figuratively. My girlfriend lived about six miles to the south, and she was excited to see me on my birthday.

As I drove on the highway through our small town—with "Sweet Emotion" by Aerosmith blasting from the radio—I noticed a tractor trailer rig on a side street to my right had cut the corner too sharp as he attempted to pull into the gas station parking lot. The back wheels of his trailer had dropped into a deep ditch, and he was stuck and not going anywhere without a tow truck. As I passed by, I spaced out as I rubbernecked at the big truck and trailer stuck in the ditch. I stared for so long that I did not notice the car directly in front of me was slowing down to make a right turn into the gas station. When I finally stopped gawking at the truck and looked forward, my heart jumped into my throat; the gap between Mom's car and the tail end of the car in front of me was rapidly closing. I jerked the steering wheel to the left to avoid a collision as the right front fender of my mom's car hit dead center into the trunk of the car in front of me.

The impact blasted the trunk open, and Christmas presents went flying and were strewn all over the highway. The collision shot the lady's vehicle into the parking lot of the gas station, and there she came to rest. It was like a scene from a movie!

It was a few weeks before Christmas, and I probably ruined it for some kid. Other motorists did their best to swerve and avoid running over the gifts scattered across both lanes of traffic. Several of the presents did not fare so well. I quickly threw the remaining joint that I had in my shirt pocket into the ditch as I walked up to see if everyone was alright. When I knew the passengers were uninjured, I headed to the gas station restroom to flush my bag of weed down the toilet. When the highway patrol arrived, a bystander told the trooper that they had seen me throw something into the ditch but couldn't tell what it was. It was dark, and fortunately for me they did not find my left-handed cigarette. There were no injuries other than totaling my mom's car and the damage to the other car. I had to cancel my date with Ella and ended up back at home for the evening. Things for sure headed south on my seventeenth birthday!

I began work at an area gas station that same year and took Arnold's old job when he started working for a used car lot in town. Back in the 1970s, most gas stations offered full service which meant that I pumped the gas, washed the windows, checked the oil and tire pressure for each customer, and would do even more if they requested it. Some requests were off limits, at least for me.

During my time at the gas station, I had a request from a very pretty, twenty-something married woman. She came in the station on numerous occasions and was always flirting with me. I was seventeen when her advances started, and she was at least twenty-five years old. My youthful, naive brain thought that she was just a pretty lady who was being nice to me. One evening while I was working alone, she pulled up to the station in her 1967 Chevy Impala to purchase a pack of cigarettes. After purchasing the cigarettes, she purposely dropped them on the floor and bent over in front of me. I thought it was an accident at first until she stood up and winked at me then walked out of the station. She was toying with my teenage mind the whole time.

The next time she came into the station, she was more forward with her advances. She walked directly up to me and put her arms around my neck and gave me a provocative French kiss. She could obviously sense my restraint—I did not want to die by the hands of an angry husband—because her words after the kiss were, "I don't think you want anything to do with this." When I stammered around trying to give her an answer, she stormed out of the station and never flirted with me again. I found out a few months later that she was hooked up with a kid younger than me. She was a lioness on the hunt, and I was one lucky antelope that somehow escaped her grasp. I felt sorry for her poor husband and wondered if he had any clue as to the type of things she was doing behind his back?

Ella and I had been a couple for close to two years. We spent a lot of time together, and being apart while she was in college, and I finished high school took a toll on our relationship. My math teacher, Mrs. Newton, told me that I needed to let her go and move on. She said long-distance relationships never last. Well, I didn't help matters by getting involved with another girl while Ella was away at college. That was the straw that broke the camel's back with her, and she ended our relationship. For years after our breakup, I dreamed about her and longed for what was such a comfort to me for so long. I woke up many a night in tears after dreaming about her and imagined what might have been!

34

Cowgirl Daze

I spent the end of my sophomore year and entire junior year dating Ella. When we split up, I realized what a loss it was. I moped around for quite some time until my interests were steered in a new direction.

Sophia lived in a town nearby, and I had seen her and talked to her on several occasions. She was friends with some of the other girls that I had dated from their same small town. This pretty cheerleader was also an avid rodeo cowgirl. I had never dated a cowgirl before, and she was very much into barrel racing horses. At the yearly rodeo in her hometown, she and other girls competed for the best time at riding their horses on a course where they circled large barrels and then galloped to the finish line. She was a barrel racing star, and I was duly impressed. When I asked her out, she had just broken up with a guy she had dated for about a year, and he still considered her his girlfriend. It didn't matter what she told him; he was not giving up on her. Knowing all of that did not dissuade me from asking her out. When he found out we were dating, I was placed at the top of his hit list. All I knew about the guy was that he was around six foot one compared to my mere five foot eight. I was at a real disadvantage and not looking forward to any confrontation.

Sophia and I had been out together on two or three separate occasions, and we liked each other well enough, and I thought the relationship might blossom if we continued to date. One Thursday night, we didn't have a date, so I was out cruising in my dad's GMC pickup. My city was dead with none of my friends out cruising, so I headed to her hometown to see what was going on there. It had a square around the courthouse, and as I cruised around the square, I noticed a group of local boys congregated at the gas station parking lot on one side of the square. Driving past with my cassette tape player blaring "Sister Golden Hair" by America, I heard someone holler at me. Because the music was so loud, I couldn't understand them.

On my next lap around the square, I pulled in and asked what was going on. Huge mistake on my part! The person hollering at me was Sophia's former beau, and he was upset with me for dating his supposed girlfriend. He shouted obscenities, and for some dumb reason I opened the door of the pickup to get out. I was never one to run from a fight even if the odds were stacked against me.

The second I opened the truck door; a fist flew directly at my face. My quick reflexes helped me avoid that first punch, and I wrapped my arms around his chest and hung on as we both fell into the front seat of my dad's pickup. After falling backward, he was on top of me and flailing his fists but could not land a single blow because of the awkward position I had him in. He was at least six feet with long arms and couldn't connect because my head was buried in his chest for protection. He also tried to shove his knee into my crotch, but at that point, I had both legs and arms wrapped around him, and he wasn't going anywhere. I continued to hang on, hoping he would wear himself out throwing those wild punches of which none were landing on me. I held on for several minutes, and he finally said, "Let me up."

Stupid me, I thought the fight was over. When I released him and we both stood up outside of the truck, he went to work on me with those long arms and big fists and landed several punches right in my face. Each time I tried to punch him, his long arms and big fists pummeled me before I could ever get close enough. It was humiliating; all his buddies cheered him on. I was wearing white overalls with my Water Buffalo hippie sandals, and my sandals were knocked off during the fight. When he finally tired of punching me in the face and cussing at me, again, I thought the fight was over. I was certainly ready for this to end, and it did as I bent over to put on my sandals. He drop-kicked me in my left eye, and I thought he'd broken my cheekbone with that swift kick to the face. The cowboy in him told me to take my long hair and hippie shoes and faggot overalls and get out of his town. Why didn't I just leave town with my dignity when I had the chance? My pride always gets me in trouble.

I climbed back into my dad's truck and headed around the square to leave town, and lo and behold, Sophia was cruising the square and stopped me to ask me what I was up to. I told her that her old boyfriend had just attacked me and did a pretty good job of it. She was angry at him and said she would talk to him. I told her it was not necessary and that I was headed home. Arriving home, my dad saw my face and how battered and bruised I was with my left eye now swollen completely shut and wanted to call the sheriff and press charges. I told him I was not pressing charges, and in the future, I had to be smarter when it came to dealing with ex-boyfriends.

Sophia and I, along with another couple, went to the state fair that weekend and everyone stared at my swollen, black-and-blue eye. Boy, was I looking good! We dated for several weeks after that, but I didn't feel like she was all that interested in me, so I stopped calling and asking her out. Looking back, I probably should have discussed it with her before giving up but that was how immature my seventeen-year-old mind was. I took quite a beating over her and that ended my short-lived cowgirl phase in a daze!

35

Double Trouble

Senior year arrived with its unique challenges. Our small school—the one I'd attended for twelve years—was to consolidate with another small school in the area and form one school district. My senior class of twelve would balloon to a whopping forty students. With all those new students, there was bound to be some new attractive cheerleaders I could ask out. The problem was most of those new girls had boyfriends, and the boyfriends intended to keep the status quo.

However, two new girls had a certain fondness for me and I for them, but their boyfriends had other plans. Alice, and her friend, Tanya, and their boyfriends enjoyed hanging out together, and I messed things up for all parties involved. Alice and Tanya both wanted to go out with me, and this caused some major consternation among their suitors. Alice's boyfriend, Tom, and I looked similar and dressed alike. We both sported long, dark brown hair and strutted around in Levi's jeans and jackets. Alice thought it was a good idea to slip a note in my back pocket while strolling in the hall before school started. She wanted to let me know how she felt and where we should meet up that evening.

Unfortunately for all involved, with so many students crowding the halls, she slipped the note into her boyfriend's back pocket, confusing him for me! He was livid to find out that she was interested in me and was willing to sneak around behind his back to be with me. His wrath was not directed at her but instead came crashing down on me. My fun senior year had become a nightmare! Tom, a few inches taller than me, was known for being a bully at his previous school. He made my life miserable the rest of the school year with insults and put downs almost daily. I couldn't wait to finally end my high school career. Tom was constantly throwing his shoulder into me in the hallway or just flat out shoving me into the wall and telling me I had better watch out.

Tanya was also interested in me but was not as outspoken about it as Alice. Somehow Tanya's boyfriend, Ben, found out she was interested in me. Tom and Ben joined forces with a singular goal: to punish me. My entire senior year I did not date either one of those girls. They would flirt with me almost every day, and both of them were notorious for sneaking up behind me in the hallway, pinching me on the butt, and then disappearing into the crowd of students. Tanya would stroll ahead of me in the hallway before school and look over her shoulder and wink at me, knowing she had my full, undivided attention.

On a warm day in late spring, Tanya wore a skimpy thin top with spaghetti straps to study hall and appeared to be a bit chilled from what I could see. She was seated directly across the table from me at arm's length. Arnold sat next to me and quietly dared me to reach across the table and pinch Tanya on one of those pencil erasers that was poking out the front of her shirt. That was another one of those moments in my past I wish I could go back and undo. Arnold's unsavory influence again brought out the stupidity in me, and I reached across the table and gave her a pinch on one of those pups' noses. Before I could retract my hand, she slapped me so hard on the face that I wore the red imprint of her right hand for the rest of the day. I immediately told her I was sorry, and she told me that was what I got for being so rude. She was right and it was the talk of the school for the rest of the week. Arnold thought it was hilarious that she smacked me so hard, and the other guys at school teased me for weeks after the incident. I was just a dumb seventeen-year-old, and in spite of all that, Tanya still wanted to go out with me.

I was to escort Tanya to our junior/senior prom because we were in the running for king and queen. She was planning to place a big kiss on me when we won, but her boyfriend and Tom were going to be there to make my life miserable. I was out-manned and out-gunned, so I skipped my senior prom. This upset Tanya because we were voted king and queen. I was not willing to die over one, perhaps really great, kiss. Tanya and I never dated, but after graduation, Alice and Tom broke up, and I dated her for a short time, but it was not meant to be or at least not meant to be permanent.

36

Hanging With Craig

My senior year, 1976, was filled with a wealth of new people in my life. Our school consolidating with another small school introduced me to a multitude of fresh faces. Craig was one of those individuals and was in Helga's junior class. He was a month older than me but in the grade below me. I started first grade at age five, and his parents had him start school at age six. We became fast friends at school, and he eventually started dating Helga. Craig was a Christian, but he still enjoyed hanging out with us partiers. He rarely cussed and never drank alcohol or smoked weed with us at parties. He was just a good guy to hang out with because he was never pushing me to get involved in questionable behavior. I was a better person when it was only the two of us. He had a positive influence on me, and I certainly needed more of that in my life.

I might have pushed him to get involved in some questionable behavior from time to time. At basketball practice after school one afternoon, Craig and I headed to the locker room before anyone else. I noticed a large, floating item in the toilet. The "Floater," as we called it, would be used for our latest prank. The victim would be Jerod, seeing that he was still in the gymnasium practicing. I instructed Craig to grab one of Jerod's socks and hold it as wide open as possible. I was going to take a large paper towel and dip said floater from the toilet without so much as touching it. Craig held the sock open and warned me not to touch him with that thing! I carefully slid the floater from the paper towel into Jerod's sock, and we left it lying with his street clothes.

Craig and I quickly changed into our street clothes and waited for the uproar to begin. The rest of the basketball team entered the locker room, talking and carrying on, and sat down next to their clothes to change. Jerod looked at his socks and said, "What the heck?" as he lifted up a very full sock. Craig and I cracked up as Jerod took a big whiff of the sock and looked at us and said, "No, you guys!"

Craig and I bolted for the nearest exit as Jerod gave chase with that sock, swinging it like he was about to throw it at us. We sprinted outside, and Jerod pursued us for three blocks until he gave up and threw the sock our way and missed. Once the sock was no longer in the equation, we all walked back to the locker room together, laughing and talking about how nasty that whole exchange was. That was gross, but it was sure entertaining! Craig and I were always pulling jokes on each other and whoever else might be handy.

Many strip pits and borrow pits could be found in the surrounding area where we lived. Coal mining created some, and the borrow pits were where the highway department removed vast amounts of rock and soil used for building the new highways near our community. Over the years, these pits filled with fifty to eighty feet of water, and we used them for swimming and/or skinny dipping late at night. The water was a pretty shade of blue because of the high levels of acidity in the pits. One especially cold winter—the temperature stayed around zero for about two weeks in January—the pits were all covered with thick ice. Or so Craig and I thought. We were bored one Saturday and decided it would be a hoot to run across the ice on a frozen-over strip pit. We parked his Camaro alongside the gravel road and took off running toward the ice. He arrived first, and I chased him to the center of the pit until the ice made this frightening cracking sound under our feet. I told Craig to keep his distance from me so that our combined weight wouldn't break the ice and send us to a certain freezing cold-water death. We both dashed for solid ground a distance from one another, with the ice popping and crackling under our feet the entire time. I genuinely thought the King of Terrors was going to take one of us out, but we somehow made it back to land and safety. Our little jaunt across the ice was about as stupid a decision as any I had made. It could have turned out so bad, and thankfully it wasn't time for either one of us to die, yet!

Craig drove a cool-looking, 1969 Chevy Camaro. His Camaro was sky blue with a black vinyl top, nice chromed Cragar wheels, and wide tires on the rear with a lift kit on the rear end that made it look really fast. I relished cruising in that car with him and listening to rock groups like ZZ Top, Lynyrd Skynyrd, Aerosmith, Fleetwood Mac, Bob Seger, Thin Lizzy, and so many others. When he started dating Helga, I was stuck riding in the backseat on our cruises. I preferred riding shotgun, and Helga was disrupting my mojo. Often while riding around in his Camaro, we had soft drinks, and when I would attempt to take a drink from my cup, Craig would gas the car so that my drink would spill all over my shirt and pants. He thought it was so funny and was always waiting and watching for his next victim. Helga fell prey to that joke on several occasions as did others.

An avid motorcyclist, Craig had been riding motorcycles since he was five years old and had gotten good at being a showoff. He was one of those guys who would pass you on the interstate going eighty miles per hour or faster while riding a wheelie! He was pretty amazing when it came to riding motorcycles. He could pop a wheelie at any speed and ride it until he was tired of showboating. Many times, Helga would be riding on the back with him, and he would pop a wheelie just to get a rise out of her. It always worked because Helga would respond with vicious slaps to the side of his motorcycle helmet in an attempt to get him to put the bike back down on both wheels. My dad never approved of Helga or any of us riding on a motorcycle. He said they were just too dangerous! I was never allowed to own one while living under Dad's roof.

Craig had two motorcycles to choose from when he rode. One bike, a Honda 125cc dirt bike, was for off road. His other motorcycle was a 750 Yamaha made for street use only. At the time, I was driving a green, 1972 Chevy Nova with a six banger in it which was certainly not the cool car that Craig cruised in.

One late night, I saw Craig and Helga riding his 750 Yamaha, and I talked him into switching rides with me for a while because I wanted to try out his bike. He agreed, and the two of them jumped into my Nova, and I climbed on his motorcycle to test drive it. We headed to the highway that ran past our small town, and I wanted to test out that Yamaha and see what it was made of. There was little to no traffic on the highway, so he and Helga tried to keep up with me as I throttled that bike up to 130 miles per hour. I slowed down, and they caught up to me, and Craig was signaling for me to slow down, which I did. When we stopped to trade back rides, he scolded me for going so fast and told me that bike could have gotten the speed shakes at that velocity, and I would have crashed. Helga had experienced speed shakes on a smaller scale while riding her bicycle as a kid. That fiasco did not end well for her. I was involved in one foolish and repeatedly dangerous situation after another. Again, someone was looking out for me and before too much longer, He would introduce Himself to me.

37

Labor Day Weekend, 1977

That weekend was a game changer for me. I had spent the better part of my teen years partying and chasing girls, and my hedonistic lifestyle was drawing to a close. I had no clue as to what was waiting for me at life's crossroad.

I still worked for my dad as a carpenter but had moved on from living with Vernie. I now lived alone in a small house that I rented in our little town. My brother was such a swine to live with, and I couldn't take the mess and the cleaning up after him any longer. He would leave his dinner plates on the coffee table for days, and mold would start growing on the old food. His alarm clock would go off right next to his head, and he wouldn't shut it off. I would walk from my bedroom at the other end of the house and shut off his alarm with him still sound asleep! The kitchen sink was always full of Vernie's dirty dishes, and I decided one day that I was done living like that and located my own place to live.

Living alone had some real advantages. I wasn't cleaning up after someone else, and meals were tailored specifically for me. With no one else to consider, I liked this new way of living. I had never lived alone and saw some real benefits when it came to social distancing.

I spent the week prior to Labor Day building metal frame walls and hanging drywall on an addition to a church in a nearby community. Craig and Cameron's husband, Peter, also worked for my dad. Craig started after he graduated high school in May, and Peter and I had been employed there for a couple of years. All of us were excited about the three-day weekend coming up and were planning on getting together on Saturday. Peter had bought a sharp looking 400cc Yamaha a few months earlier. I had purchased a 125cc Kawasaki enduro two weeks prior, and the three of us wanted to go riding on Saturday near a large lake in our area. We planned on meeting at my parents' house, Green Acres, at ten o'clock that Saturday morning and riding our motorcycles the six miles to the lake, which was near the tiny house in the woods—the first place that I called home.

Peter stopped by my bachelor pad on his way to my parents' house. I asked him if he wanted me to take a doobie or two with us for fun. He said we wouldn't need any of that, and dirt bike riding would provide plenty of excitement without it. He headed off to my parents' house, and I told him I would be there in a few minutes. My motorcycle was dripping gas near the shut-off valve, and I wanted to check it out before leaving. I had to shut my gas off each time I turned the motorcycle off or it would constantly drip gasoline. I couldn't figure out what was wrong with my shut-off valve, so I headed off to see my parents. Upon arriving, I shut off the gas on my bike and went into the house. Peter and Craig were raring to go and tired of waiting on me. I said, "Let's go," and we headed out the door to mount our metal steeds. Helga followed us out the door, and Craig gave her a kiss good-bye. At that point in their relationship, they were very near to becoming engaged. Peter and I teased Craig because he just had to get one last kiss in before we headed out. That statement would prove to be prophetic, considering only one of us would return home that evening.

The three of us took off from my dad's place in search of fun and adventure. We were riding on the blacktop highway that ran past Green Acres when my motorcycle died about a mile down the road, and Peter and Craig kept going because they didn't see that I had stopped. I stood there by the side of the road, trying to figure out what was wrong with my motorcycle. My buds finally noticed that I was missing, turned around, and came back to see what had happened. As they pulled up, I remembered that I had shut off my gas line when I stopped at my parents' house. I turned the gas line back on and voilà, my motorcycle started. We headed out again on our way to the lake.

Forgetting to turn my gas back on would prove to have some serious, unintended consequences. We were all being safe, wearing helmets, riding single file, and not exceeding the speed limit. Being cautious was not enough when God's providence is steering you toward a life-altering event that I was destined to participate in. We rode about four miles on the blacktop and were a couple of miles from the lake when we approached a hilltop riding single file. The first thing I saw as we neared the top of the hill was a car coming toward us at an angle and in our lane of traffic.

Peter swerved his motorcycle to the right to avoid being hit head-on. He missed the front fender of that car by maybe an inch as he headed down into the ditch at about fifty miles per hour, trying to stop. I was next in line and had only enough time to turn the front wheel of my bike to the right and was struck by the driver's side front bumper and fender on the left side of my bike, starting at the gas tank and on to the rear of the bike. It was a miracle that it didn't rip my entire left leg off! I remember being shot up in the air about eight feet before I landed flat on my back in the ditch. I sat up and my left foot was lying in my lap; I was looking at the bottom of my heavy-duty leather work boot.

My leg was broken above and below the knee, and my left foot was crushed after having been smashed between the motorcycle and the front bumper of the car. Peter finally stopped and turned around and headed back toward me. He saw me sitting up in the ditch and briefly stopped to see if I was all right. I told him my leg was broken and asked if he would please straighten it out so blood flow wouldn't be so restricted. My left leg was a twisted-up mess! With a shaky voice he said he couldn't do that and headed back behind me. I wondered what he was doing and why wasn't he helping me?

During the brief time that he was gone, I raised myself up on my elbows and proceeded to pull my broken body backward in the ditch in an attempt to straighten out my leg, even just a little. As I pulled my body backward in the ditch, my left foot dropped off my lap, and I was able to somewhat undo the gnarled mess that was my leg and foot. Peter knew I was at least moving and alive, but he could see behind me that Craig was not moving at all. Peter came back and informed me, while in tears, that Craig was dead. My first thought was that he was a Christian and was in a better place. He and his motorcycle took a direct hit. Craig's body and motorcycle were still wedged under the front of that car when it came to rest in the ditch. What a tragic, heartbreaking event. The county coroner's report later stated that the crash broke nearly every bone in his body and the cause of death was blunt force trauma.

My leg and foot didn't hurt at first because I was in shock. It took the ambulance at least thirty minutes to arrive, and by that time, the pain had found me out. Believe it or not, my dad was in the area and just happened upon the crash. He had no idea that it was his son, son-in-law, and future son-in-law who were involved. Dad walked up to me, and the first thing I said to him was how sorry I was for buying a motorcycle and ignoring his cautionary advice. He had warned me over and over that I shouldn't put myself in harm's way by riding a motorcycle. I somehow knew everything at age eighteen and refused his wise counsel. I burst into tears; I felt so awful that this had happened and that my good friend was now dead. If I hadn't forgotten to turn my gas back on, this would never have happened. The time spent stopped and turning my gas back on made us arrive at that hill just in time to meet that car on our side of the road.

The trip in the ambulance to the nearest hospital was awful. The paramedics placed my broken left leg and foot into a blow-up boot to stabilize my leg until we arrived at the emergency room. They refused to give me anything for pain until the doctors examined me and had taken some X-rays of my leg and foot. Every single bump on that highway sent new levels of pain through me as we made the thirty-minute drive to the ER in one of the towns near us.

Upon arriving at the hospital, my parents and other family members joined me as they rushed me inside. Several nurses and staff members moved my broken body from the gurney to an exam table, and I cried and screamed through the whole process! By that point, I was begging for some pain meds, but they again refused, sighting my need for X-rays and an examination by the attending physician. After being X-rayed, the doctor came in to examine my leg and foot. My left leg was broken just above the knee and again about six inches above my ankle. My left foot had been crushed across all the bones in the middle of my foot. The talk was that they might have to amputate my foot if it couldn't be repaired. The bone going to my big toe was then located over the top of the other bones in my foot.

I had no pain meds at this point, and the doctor grabbed my left ankle and gave my leg an excruciating yank to straighten it up a bit and stabilize it for the trip to Little Rock. I went ballistic! I made every attempt I could to kick that doctor with my good leg while three nurses and other staff members did all they could to hold me down. Then the doctor started pushing the broken bone from my big toe that was on top of the other bones, back into place, and I did all that I could to stop him by kicking and pleading with him to quit. With so many nerves in my foot, it was painful beyond words. I don't remember if the doctor accomplished his task or just gave up because I was in such pain, but either way, he ultimately stopped. When they finally gave me some pain meds, I calmed down and was much more compliant.

My dear mother rode with me in the ambulance to Little Rock. We arrived about two hours later, and I was still in a fog from the pain shot. They rushed me into surgery as soon as the operating room opened up, but I still landed on a gurney waiting for quite some time. I vividly remember those hot blankets that were placed on me while waiting and how good they felt. When I finally had surgery, they set the bones in my lower leg and pinned all the bones in my foot back together with stainless steel pins and put a cast on the lower part of my leg. I had to be placed in traction and lie flat on my back for a solid week because of the break above my knee. The orthopedic surgeon drilled a hole through the bone just below my knee; inserted a stainless-steel rod through the hole that extended out a few inches on each side of my knee and attached ropes on each side that went up and over a pulley at the end of the bed. Then weights were attached to the ropes at the end of the bed. This was to pull my femur back into place before my next surgery about a week later. The weights would pull and slide me down in the bed, and the nurses would slide me back up in the bed several times each day.

After traction the surgeon operated on me again and inserted a stainless-steel rod into the bone above my knee and then placed a plaster cast on that, covering my entire leg and foot. All I could do while lying there in bed for seven days was to look heavenward. The Lord had wounded me in order to heal me. Previously, when thoughts of death would enter my mind, I cast them aside and refused to stare death in the face. I was forced to consider and meditate on how short this life could be and realized that I was not invincible. My dear friend was a mere eighteen years old, and his poor parents would have to plan his funeral. How awful that must have been for them! The Lord had broken my proud heart into a million pieces, and only He could heal it.

My parents spent as much time as they could at the medical center with me. I had three separate surgeries and spent eighteen days in the hospital. My dad's only sister, who was a Christian, spent many afternoons just sitting by my bedside while silently reading in her Bible. I was sure she was praying that God would have mercy on my soul. Her prayers and the prayers of many others were answered when God gave me a new heart and life. I was changed forever as God enabled me to repent of my sins and trust in Jesus Christ to the saving of my soul! Hallelujah, what a Savior! The weight of guilt that my sins had produced was removed as I saw by faith that Jesus Christ had paid in full that infinite debt I owed to God because of my sin and rebellion. His death on the cross rendered a full payment to God for the sins that I had committed. The perfect life that Jesus lived was put to my account, and, through faith in Him, I possessed that perfect righteousness God's law required. I was set free from the darkness that had plagued my soul and once enslaved me to the sinful inclinations of my prideful heart. I could at long last walk in the light of His glorious grace, desiring to please Him with each and every step. Before conversion, I had no real desire to please God and lived only for myself. I loved my sin and was always ready to dive in headfirst when devilish opportunities presented themselves.

Along with a believing heart, I was given a whole new set of challenges in dealing with what remained of that sinful nature within all of us. After conversion, I no longer loved but hated my sin and everything about it. The chief desire of my heart after believing was to live for God and please Him above all else. The desire of my heart was to never sin again. God would soon show me that my sinful nature was not yet totally eradicated, and it wouldn't be until I entered His presence in heaven. Before my journey through this world ends, there are many more foolish situations that I would place myself in and some deep dark valleys that I would and will continue to struggle with on my travels home!

To be continued...

.

Made in the USA
Las Vegas, NV
20 February 2024